**"I was crazy a while, and then I wasn't,
and then I was. That's how it went."**

At the age of seventy-four, Ellis Burt—Georgia sharecropper's son and ex-convict—remembers a simple life that unfolded against the complex, ever-changing background of the American South, from the Depression through the difficult birth of Civil Rights. In his time he loved deeply and sired a son—only to inadvertently bring ruin upon his family and himself through a tragic weakness of spirit. This is Ellis Burt's story, told in his own earnest yet unassuming words—the penance of a man of uncommon personal dignity striving for the peace he fervently craves...as he drifts toward the salvation he feels he does not merit.

A novel of remarkable poignancy and power, Judson Mitcham's *The Sweet Everlasting* carries on the rich Southern literary tradition of Faulkner, Welty, and Carson McCullers. It is a story of damnation and surprising redemption; a singular novel that painfully and enthrallingly reveals the heart and soul of a good but flawed man.

"A rare pleasure...
scenes so shimmering and vivid they lodge
in memory...a bone-deep story, felt as well as told...
Judson Mitcham's first novel is spare, muted, painful,
funny, and raw."
—*Newark Star-Ledger*

"A writer of great heart, intelligence,
and psychological insight...*The Sweet Everlasting* puts me
in mind of Cormac McCarthy's writing."
—Hilma Wolitzer, author of *Tunnel of Love*

"A remarkable novel...Mitcham's characters
are vividly realized, and his depiction of the rural South
is both sweet and savage, but the voice of Ellis Burt,
homespun yet lyrical, is a work of art."
—*Booklist*

THE SWEET EVERLASTING

JUDSON MITCHAM

AN AVON BOOK

AVON BOOKS, INC.
1350 Avenue of the Americas
New York, New York 10019

The University of Georgia Press hardcover edition contains the following Library of Congress Cataloging in Publication Data:

Mitcham, Judson.
   The sweet everlasting : a novel / by Judson Mitcham.
      p.   cm.
   1. Men—Georgia—Fiction. I. Title
PS3563.I7356S94   1996
813'.54—dc20   95-24474

First Bard Printing: January 2000
First Avon Books Mass Market Paperback Printing: September 1997

BARD TRADEMARK REG. U.S. PAT. OFF. AND IN OTHER COUNTRIES, MARCA REGISTRADA, HECHO EN U.S.A.

Printed in the U.S.A.

OPM 10 9 8 7 6 5 4 3 2 1

For my mother

"All flesh is grass,
and all the goodliness thereof
is as the flower of the field . . ."
Isaiah 40:6

THE SWEET
EVERLASTING

1

It was an idea as real as a sharp stick, and even better for drawing blood. But if you looked at it good, like I finally did, it didn't have nothing to back it up.

Out of a six-year-and-two-month sentence to the state prison at Milledgeville, I served it all—August 1954 to October 1960. I was crazy a while, and then I wasn't, and then I was. That's how it went. One second I'd be a free man—with Susan beside me and the boy on my lap—and the next I'd be awake on my back and looking up into the dirty light coming through my cell window.

The day they let me out, I walked on down the road and sat under a tree, and I remember how when the wind picked up, leaves started to fall. I'm seventy-four years old now, and that was a long time ago, like it was another life. But some of what happened before that morning, every now and then it seems like yesterday.

2

Mr. Stillwell had eight families working his land, five white and three black. His land was broke up into two parts—one of them right there at his house, where we had our farm and where a black family by the name of Cutts had one, and then there was another big piece about four miles down the road, the other side of Yellow

Shoals and halfway to Ricksville. We didn't hardly ever see the families who worked that land, except maybe at church and at school. Some of them went to school over in Ricksville and some at Yellow Shoals, where I went.

Mr. Stillwell was the richest man in the county. He had all that land, but then he owned the bank and most of the stores in town too. To look at him, you wouldn't have thought he was a rich man. He always dressed real plain. He'd wear brown work clothes or overalls. He'd got his money farming—at least that's how his family had got their money; it was passed down to Mr. Stillwell— and he wanted folks to look at him like he was a farmer. But if you did look close at him, you might see a crease in his work clothes, and you wouldn't find no blood or dirt or grease on his overalls, or where they'd been mended from being snagged on a barbwire fence. He had the cleanest work clothes this side of the Sears and Roebuck catalog. Looked like a uniform.

He was a short man, wiry and thin, and he walked with a strut. I used to make Mama and Daddy laugh by imitating how he walked. He'd stick out his rear end and jut his head forward and pull his arms back all at the same time, so he looked real stiff, and then he'd sort of strut.

His hair was pure white, but then one day when he come down to our house to tell Daddy to do something, he took off his hat and his hair was black as tarpaper. Daddy stood out in the front room talking to him, but me and Mama eased on into the back of the house, went back in the bedroom and fell out. Mama stuffed a pillow in her mouth so she wouldn't honk. After a while we settled down, but then when Mr. Stillwell left and Daddy walked in and we seen the expression on his face, we fell out again, and Daddy with us.

4

Mr. Stillwell had three girls—one that was four years older than me, one that was my age, named Alice, and one that was a baby. I didn't hardly ever see them. They stayed right around the house, and I didn't go up there much. Alice was in my grade at school, and I seen her there. She was always real nice to me. She knew my daddy worked for hers, but then so did half the county, so that didn't mean much. Her folks always sent somebody to pick her up after school, and sometimes they'd pass me while I was walking home, and Alice would always smile and wave at me. She was a friendly girl, and I liked her a lot. She never let on that she thought she was better than anybody else.

Which is to say she wasn't nothing like her daddy. Uncle Mack use to sit and listen to him down at Hodges Store, where they called Mr. Stillwell "The Judge," like a lot of other folks did, even though he hadn't ever been a judge and wasn't even a lawyer. The word was that the governor had wanted to make him a district judge one time, but Mr. Stillwell had turned him down.

The Judge liked to talk about his family history. He'd tell it over and over, and we'd hear the stories when Uncle Mack come out to our house. It wasn't like Uncle Mack had any business being on close speaking terms with Mr. Stillwell. It was just that Mr. Stillwell liked to talk in front of a crowd, and he could usually find him one down at Hodges Store.

They said Mr. Stillwell's granddaddy had rode with Nathan Bedford Forrest in the War Between the States, rode with him most of the war, they said, at Shiloh and at Chickamauga. There was a tintype of his granddaddy standing beside the general, and I know that's a true fact since Alice brung it to school one day to show it off. It was a bent old tintype, smudged and hard to make out—two men in uniform standing by one another, and one of them was supposed to be her great-granddaddy and the other one the general.

Folks said there was a room inside Mr. Stillwell's house where they had his granddaddy's war things all laid out, like in a museum, everything in glass cases.

The Confederate statue on the courthouse square over in Ricksville had his granddaddy's name chiseled in at the bottom as the one who give the money for it. Mr. Stillwell would point out how the statue was turned due south, even though that made the soldier face sideways to the street. He said that was done by order of his granddaddy, who wanted the statue to show its backside to the North for the rest of eternity.

There was a time when I used to wonder about that room in Mr. Stillwell's house, the one with all the war things in it, wondered what it looked like. I'd been over there with my daddy, but I'd never been inside the house, and as far as I could tell, neither had my daddy. He'd stand out in the back yard while Mr. Stillwell spoke to him from off the porch about business matters—seed and fertilizer and such. It was clear that Mr. Stillwell wouldn't let no sharecroppers set foot in his house. He didn't even want you on his porch.

Once when there was a hog-killing and all the families that worked for him come over to help out with it like always, one of the little white girls from down the road, about seven years old, she went up and sat in a rocking chair on the back porch. Mr. Stillwell shot a look at the girl's mama, who run up there and told the girl to get herself down from there; said didn't nobody ask her up on the porch.

After the hog-killing was over, we'd always have us a big supper out in the back yard—some of the best stew you ever ate in your life. There'd be these long two-by-eights laid across sawhorses to make tables, and we'd serve ourselves and then sit down around the tables to eat. The three black families took their plates and sat under the chinaberry tree about thirty yards off from the tables. Didn't nobody tell them to do that; didn't nobody have to.

But then didn't all the white families eat at the same place either. Mr. Stillwell and his wife and their girls all took their plates and went up on the porch and sat by themselves.

My daddy had a granddaddy in the war too, but he never talked about it much. Said he got put in a prison camp up in Chicago and that he walked back to Georgia after the war.

He served as a regular private, a foot soldier, but one day they pulled him into a field hospital to help them out, and they made him hold men down while they sawed off their legs or arms.

My daddy said sometimes, out of the blue, his granddaddy just cried and shook; said his mama told him a story that he never heard his granddaddy tell, about how they went charging up a hill, and the man in front of him got shot in the head and the man's ear flew off and landed in my great-granddaddy's mouth. Said he spit it out and stood there with it in his hand, looking at it, and he didn't know what to do with it—whether to lay it down on the dead man or not—and then he put it in his pocket and went on up the hill.

Daddy said there was a parade one time, long after the war, and they tried to get his granddaddy to march in it, but he crawled in the bed and he wouldn't get out.

7

3

My daddy had them little strokes before he died. One night he come in from the field and wasn't himself, come to the table with his shirt off—the same man that always liked to wash up good before supper and might even put on a clean shirt if he had one. That evening when he sat down, he just started to eat right off, never said the blessing. That's what scared Mama so bad.

Daddy didn't remember none of it the next day, even laughed about what a fool he must have looked like, sitting there barechested at the table. But you could tell it got off with him. He grabbed Mama and wrestled her into a hug, said she knew he was a crazy man when she married him, now didn't she? They held onto each other for a little bit, standing like that, like a couple between dances waiting for another slow tune to start up. But then when Daddy walked on ahead of me out towards the field I seen how his right foot was lazy, and I yelled out and asked him what was wrong with his leg, but he didn't answer.

My daddy was a quiet man all his life. He used to say if a man talked a lot you just listen to him long enough and most likely you'll find out he don't know which end of the mule to feed sugar to. What words my daddy did use, he was big on using right. He didn't use no blue language, not unless it was called for, but then he knew how to turn it loose.

And I remember one time I said I hated rutabagas, and he said well maybe I didn't like them much, but I didn't hate them. He said you don't go around hating vegetables like you had a grudge against them and was going to get even.

Daddy couldn't read or write, and he was ashamed of it. He never tried to use a word he didn't know, and the ones he did know, he thought about them a lot, trying to make sure he was right. Sometimes he asked me to look up a word for him in the big dictionary they had at school, but he made me promise not to tell nobody about it. Usually it was a word he'd heard somebody use, maybe in town or over at the store, and that it looked like everybody knew but him. I'd write down what the dictionary said, every bit of it, and when I brung it home, Mama would read it out loud, and sometimes it cleared things up, and sometimes it didn't. I wish I could remember some of the words now, but I can't.

The early morning was my daddy's favorite part of the day. That's when he liked to sit on the front steps with a cup of black coffee, and I remember him drinking that coffee and pointing things out to me, like one time when he nodded toward the fence where a crow had lighted. "Ellis, look yonder," I remember him saying, "the sun on them wings."

Then one morning he woke up and couldn't move. Had his eyes open, and he was breathing but couldn't move, and there was this awful scared look in his eyes, and that night we lost him.

The day we buried him it hadn't rained in a long time and the red clay was packed hard. I went over to where they'd opened the grave, and I looked down into the hole, and I looked over at the pile of dirt beside it, and that dirt got to me. They planned to put my daddy down in the hole, and then throw dirt on top of him—all that red dirt I could see piled up—pack it down on top of him, and that's where he'd be from then on. They'd dressed him up, and they'd laid him out in a fancy box, but they planned to put him in a hole like he was a dog, so he wouldn't stink.

Mama come and took me by the hand and led me away. They'd said the prayers and was fixing to lower him down, and we wasn't supposed to watch that, but they started before we got out of the graveyard, and I turned back and I seen him go under, and then I

9

looked up at the other folks standing there, and I looked past the tombstones and out across the road, looked over into the pasture at some cows, and it hit me then how even them fool cows was still alive but my daddy was dead. The cows would be eating and sleeping and waking up to the light and the sweet air, and all the while my daddy would be dead.

I got to thinking the other day how long I've outlived him already, wondering if I started to give out like that, who'd take care of me, since I ain't got nobody that really loves me, like me and Mama did him.

I had somebody once, though. First time I seen her, I was working for a traveling fair, setting up the Tilt-A-Whirl. We'd stopped down near Jesup and raised everything up on a dirt patch some folks thought was too close to a church, and I reckon it was, but that church stayed dark all week long. I don't know who we was supposed to be bothering, except maybe the dead in that graveyard by the church, and I had a feeling they was on our side.

When I looked at Susan that first time, I didn't have a clue, though it's a fact that she could have been a picture in a book. I mean, she stood out right away from everybody around her—blackest hair I'd ever seen on a white woman, and dark eyes.

She was standing over by Chubby McElhannon's shooting gallery. I got the ride going and then I looked over, and there she was. I stopped the ride, let the folks out, locked the others in, started it up, and she was still there, still none of my concern, but I seen her, and I noticed she never did talk to nobody. I set them up again, and when I turned back this time, she was gone.

Just past the spot where she'd been standing, I seen Chubby leaning over the front of his booth, waving and yelling at everybody that walked by to come over. There was lots of folks for him to shout at, this being about the time the Japanese surrendered and everybody still celebrating. I seen Chubby shouting and yapping, talking fast as he could, calling people names he made up for them, usually not real nice. Might call a soldier in uniform "Hero" or "General," or a girl with a candy apple "Sticky Lips." And when all I seen was Chubby being his fat self, I reckoned the girl had give up on whoever she was probably waiting for, but it didn't make no difference to me.

Sunday morning, like always, we broke down everything and got it all loaded on the trucks. And like always, there was townfolks standing off to the side watching us. Some of them had walked over from that little church, mostly children in their good clothes. And then you had folks who come out there to walk and crawl across the fairgrounds after we left, looking for dropped money in the sawdust and dirt. Never seen a town where they didn't show up. Crawford, the man who run the freak show, he called them the buzzards. We never did let them get going till we started to pull out. They just got in the way and made the work dangerous—folks everywhere down on their knees or wandering around, looking at the ground and not at where they're going, and us working fast and moving some pieces so heavy they don't give nobody a second chance.

That's where I seen Susan again, out there with the buzzards. She had her hair tied back, and something about that—I can't rightly say what—made her look like some kind of movie star. What I mean is, she was that good-looking.

I never was a man to just go up and talk to a woman, and that was even more true if she was good-looking. Made me feel like I had a big sign hung around my neck, and she could take one look at me and know everything, and then I'd be a fool. But I studied

Susan as close as I could without letting her know it. I remember she had on a plain cotton dress, yellow, and she had on heavy brown shoes that was beat-up and scuffed. She stood off to the side by herself.

I guess that would have been all I ever knew about her if it hadn't been for them new boys we had picked up down in Waycross. Don't even remember their names now, just that one was red-headed and loudmouthed and the other one was big and slow and done whatever his buddy told him. I'd gone across to the other side of the field, and when I come back I seen them two boys with Susan, the big one sort of blocking her off from the rest of the folks out there, and the boy with red hair leaning up close and talking to her real sweet-like and smiling. And then he started to touch her, rubbed his hand up her arm and let it come sideways across her chest and stay there. He put his other hand on her thigh and pulled up on her dress. Susan knocked his hands off and tried to twist away, but the big one had her in his grip, with one hand grabbed onto her dress and pulling at it, and his other arm coming around across her stomach, holding her tight. I could see her mouth moving and I reckoned she was cussing them for all she was worth, but two trucks had revved up close by, both with bad mufflers, and I couldn't hear nothing.

Here it was, broad daylight, and there's maybe thirty folks standing there, and they know what's happening—this girl being held and felt-up right in front of them. They know what they're seeing, but they don't do nothing. They look away, act like it's none of their business.

Now that told me something, but I didn't know exactly what till a long time later. Right then what I seen was two boys that hadn't been working for the fair more than a week, and that decided they'd take a little break while the rest of us was straining our guts out trying to get on the road, and on top of that, they was going to get hot all over this girl right out there in the open.

And I can't deny I already seen Susan as connected to me somehow, since I'd been watching her and thinking on who she might be and saying to myself how pretty she was.

I picked up a crowbar and walked up behind the big boy. I hit him where his backbone went into his neck, and he went down, and then I turned to the other one. Now I'd done dropped this boy's goon buddy, lots bigger than he was, and I come at him with the crowbar, but all he wanted to do was keep on getting his hands all over the girl. When I come at him he picked her up and swung her in my direction. But Susan had a hand on his face, clawing it with her fingernails, going for his eyes, so when he swung her at me and tried to wheel out of my way, he wasn't seeing too good. I ducked around and caught him with the crowbar on the side of his knee, and that's all it took—one good shot of real pain and he went down, howling and crying. Both of them boys whined and snuffled like babies. And I remember how they looked at me, like "What's got into you?" Like I done something they couldn't begin to make sense of.

Susan's dress was tore all down the front, just barely hanging on her, and she didn't have nothing much on underneath. I don't know exactly what I expected, but she'd done picked up a good-size rock, and she held it in her right hand, held her torn dress together with her left.

When I turned in her direction, she said, "Mister, you take one step at me and I'll bust your head wide open."

Now the two Waycross boys was groaning and cussing, coming up off the ground. I didn't know if I was going to have to fight them. Turned out they just wanted to get away, both of them being your ordinary cowards, ready to pick on a little girl but scared of anybody else, scared of the girl too, if the truth be told. But I seen the boy with red hair look up when she said that to me. His face was still all twisted, but I seen a flash of something else, seen it in his eyes when he started to get up, like he was laughing at me. I swung my boot between his legs and kicked him right in his future.

I've swallowed a lot in my life, but I never could abide nobody laughing at me. Folks cuss you and call you every name they know, and that's one thing, but when they start laughing, that's different. I mean when something about you has struck somebody else as downright foolish, and they don't have no more control over it than if they had swallowed some bad food and it was coming up on them. That's what I never could stand.

But it wasn't just the laughing. I never could stand going along thinking things was one way and then finding out they was another. It always give me that feeling I got one time when I was a boy and I stepped on what I thought was solid ground and it turned out to be some rotted planks with weeds hiding them, and I fell straight into the hole a outhouse used to sit over. I crawled out of there itching for somebody to fight.

When I looked back, Susan was a good thirty yards off already, headed out across the fairgrounds, walking fast. I just went back to work, thinking she was another one of them things that don't make no sense and that it don't make no sense to worry about neither.

Imagine how surprised I was when I seen her that afternoon. We had pulled into Brunswick to set up, and she was sitting in the doorway of old Mrs. Kilgore's trailer, eating a piece of fried chicken. Come to find out later on that Mrs. Kilgore had seen

Susan running across the fairgrounds crying and holding her dress together, and she'd grabbed her and taken her into the trailer and pinned up the dress. Hadn't asked, just ordered the girl inside, which is the kind of lady she was.

When I seen Susan in that trailer, I just looked at her and kept walking, figured she was best left alone. It turned out she'd taken up with Mrs. Kilgore, but right at first she didn't hardly come out of the trailer at all. Mrs. Kilgore worked one of the hot dog and sausage stands, and later on Susan cooked for her, but for about that first week didn't nobody much know she was there.

Then one evening I come across her when I was walking out taking me a smoke. Looked like she had the same idea. It was near dark and we was coming towards one another on a dirt road that cut behind the fairgrounds. From way off, I knew exactly who she was.

It had quit raining not too long before, and you could hear the rain still falling in the trees, and you could smell it in the dirt—a sweet smell with a edge to it, like a root when you crack it open and put it up to your nose.

I didn't know what to expect, seeing as how the last time we spoke she'd promised to bust open my skull with a rock. I found out later on that Mrs. Kilgore had talked about me some, had told her I wasn't a bad sort. When I got near to where Susan was, I froze up, like I do. We nodded and then we both just stood there.

"Nice evening," she said.

"Yeah, it's turned off right nice," I said.

There was many a night ahead of us when we would walk out after supper, and she'd point things out to me, things I'd never noticed or knew the names of, things her Aunt Lenora, who was the woman that raised her, had taken time to show her.

Susan knew the names of every flower and weed, every tree, and if a sweet smell rose up on the breeze, she knew where it come from. That first evening, I seen that she was holding her cigarette in her right hand and a pretty little white flower in the other, and I asked her what she had there.

She lifted it up and looked at it, then looked back at me. "Just catfoot," she said, "or some call it sweet everlasting." And I nodded like that meant something to me.

We walked on back to the fairgrounds together, and it was like we was both fighting something off. There's a way folks walk—a man and a woman—when they're more interested in being together than in getting to where they're going. They sort of weave all over the place, stop and start again. But we didn't walk that way; we stepped off towards the trailers like we had work to do that wouldn't wait.

I knew better than to ask too many questions. There would come a time when Susan told me all about it—why she just took off and come with us, why she was ready to hit me with that rock, but it would take her a while to start to talk to me.

And I won't tell the whole story here either. Just say that between that evening when we met up on the dirt road and about a month later things happened that made some kind of difference to her, and late one night just before she disappeared into Mrs. Kilgore's trailer, Susan pulled me to her and kissed me on the mouth. And five months later we got married, and we took our honeymoon like kids, riding every ride the fair had, all by ourselves and in the dark after everybody else had gone. I paid a boy to come along and set us up and turn us off. Susan said it was the most romantic thing she'd ever seen, but it wasn't, I know that. Still, here was these rides I was sick of, and all at once, because of her, I was out of my head like a eight-year-old, riding them with her that night.

I woke up before she did the next morning, and from where I was laying I could look out the window and across a weed field, and I could see mist drifting along, shapes that sort of leaned sideways and eased off real slow and disappeared. Little bodies of haze—what a ghost might look like to somebody that ain't ever seen one.

After we got married, me and Susan settled down in Red Oak. I got work hauling bobbins in a cotton mill, and Susan, she started doing housecleaning for folks, which she said she'd done before. We got us a place in the mill village, a little frame house like all the others.

Back in them days, the mill blew a whistle, like a train whistle, only louder, to tell folks it was almost time for the shift to change, and then in a half hour they blew it again and you was supposed to be there, on the job. Over the years I worked every shift, but right after we married I worked the first, which meant getting up at five.

Susan and me, we liked to cook together. I'd make the coffee and fry bacon or ham or fatback, and Susan, she cooked the eggs and grits and biscuits. Truth is, I was as good a cook as she was, but she wouldn't let me do nothing but what she said I couldn't mess up.

We'd be sitting at the table when the first whistle blew, and that was our signal to finish up. We'd have us one more cup of coffee—we both liked it strong—and then we'd clean off the table, and she'd fix me up something for later on, like a ham and biscuit.

When I turned down Third Street, a thin glow would be coming over the pines. And then I'd hear the mill humming and making that low rasping sound that went higher when you stepped inside and then higher if you opened the door to where the spinning frames were. When you come in on the bottom floor, you had to go through the machine shop to get to the stairs. I used to see old Foy Pirkle over there by his lathe every morning. He'd have a cheek full of tobacco, and he'd grin that brown grin and put his thumb up when I went by. The shop smelled like oil and hot steel, and then when you went past it, out towards the loading docks, you could smell the raw cotton that the heisters would be hauling in.

If you went on up into the weave shop, everything was louder and faster and the air was different. There was 392 looms in there, booming and clacking, and you could feel the floor shake, and since the looms all moved on their own, the place looked like it was in some kind of wild hurry. The overhead pipes sprayed out mist, so the shop always had a hazy look to it, and it had a little bit of a sweet smell, not as sweet as the cloth room, but just a hint. And the noise would knock you down. They had deaf folks all over the weave shop. You'd hear them yelling at each other outside on their break.

From the first week, I had my eyes set on a job as a loom-fixer, the best-paying job in the mill, short of being a shift boss. Everybody knew the loom-fixers could get jobs anywhere there was a cotton mill. Can't everybody learn it, they said.

Don't get me wrong. I didn't have no problem with hauling bobbins. It was honest work, but I knew I could probably get me some machines to run or fix, and then I'd get paid better, and maybe my back wouldn't hurt so bad.

Turned out you had to practically know the governor to get trained as a loom-fixer. When I went up and asked a shift boss about it, he laughed at me and waved a man over and shouted it to him and they both laughed. I asked them what was so damn funny, and the shift boss said, "Boy, you don't know nothing." He pointed out across the floor. "Take a look at the folks working them looms. Lots of them wants to be loom-fixers, and they can't, and they know what a loom by God *is*. You ain't hardly ever seen one."

They looked at each other and laughed, and right then was when I made up my mind I'd be a loom-fixer.

After my shift was done, I'd hang around and watch, mostly Jamey Phillips, about the oldest loom-fixer there, and he never minded it. Didn't say much though, so I had to look real close. And he was so deaf that if I did shout him a question he might not even know it.

I watched him for about two months, and then one day somebody was out, and they didn't have nobody else, and they pulled me off bobbins to try to help out, and I guess I done all right. And then when this man on third shift broke his neck driving drunk, instead of training somebody new, they put me on.

Third shift was hard. I couldn't get my sleep right, and I blew up at Susan a few times about nothing, which she didn't take kindly to, to say the least. She had a temper herself. Said she didn't need *no* man, would do fine on her own. Said if I thought I could even begin to speak to her just any way I wanted to, she'd be more than happy to pack up her things and let me have my precious life all to myself. And one more thing, she said: when she was gone, she was gone. None of this coming and going for her. End of the line, as far as she was concerned.

Now I myself have never been one to push folks around, but then I never much cared to be around folks I knew I could do it to either. Susan was pretty much the same way, and so we always had a lot of fights. But we got used to it, even laughed about it, and I don't believe we ever really tried to hurt one another.

And third shift wasn't such a bad setup. I'd get home before she left for work in the morning, and she'd have already cooked breakfast, and we'd eat and talk a while before she left for her cleaning jobs, about the middle of the morning. I'd stay up till around noon-time, doing things around the house or looking at a newspaper. I used to work in her flower garden some. And then I'd go to sleep, and I'd be in the bed when she come home.

She'd take her a long bath and then come out and crawl in the bed with me and wake me up curving against me, all smooth and warm, while the last rays of the sun streamed in past the curtains like it was sunrise, only the light would be dying away.

I've had my troubles, but I know there must be whole lives that go by without having anything as sweet as what we had then. I'd be halfway in a dream when Susan would touch me and draw me to her, and while the day went over into the night, we'd give up everything that was in us.

Back when Susan was still living with Mrs. Kilgore, we used to go for long walks or she'd come over and sit beside me while I run the Tilt-A-Whirl, and back then Susan had these questions about everything. I wasn't nobody to ask, and I believe she knew that, since I didn't even get to high school. What I figure is that she seen I wasn't going to look at her funny and make her feel foolish or ashamed, whatever she said. And it wasn't my job to answer the questions, just to listen to them.

I remember her bringing me over a sausage dog one day, fixed up the way she liked it but I didn't much care for—mustard and onions and Tabasco on it. The Tilt-A-Whirl had broke down, and I had took the motor apart but couldn't fix it, since it needed this belt we didn't have. And so she come over with the food and some Co-Colas, and we found us a place in the shade, and sat back, and there was a nice breeze blowing, and I remember that was when she asked me how you could ever know if you was awake or dreaming, since a dream can make you feel like it really is happening, but then when you wake up, you know you been dreaming. Her question was this: after you wake up, how do you know you ain't going to wake up again? How do you ever know for sure everything ain't a dream?

Of course, I couldn't answer, but I think Susan valued the serious look I could hold onto while she talked about such things. And I think she liked the fact that I wouldn't say nothing that tried to set the question to rest too easy, like "Well, I guess if the good Lord had wanted us to know that, he'd have give us a way to figure it out."

Susan liked to talk about all sorts of things, like dreams and the stars and what all was down at the bottom of the ocean, and she wanted to know if time could have a beginning or a end. And if it did have, she said, how was anybody supposed to understand what was on either side of it? And after we had decided on getting married, she wanted to know if there was any plan to people's lives. What if she had never took that walk? she wanted to know, and what if the Waycross boys had never jumped on her or if I'd been working on the other side of the fairgrounds at the time? She wanted to know if everything was just luck.

During those days, and later on too, I liked to sit back and just look at her, and I noticed lots of things. Like sometimes, for no reason, she'd go over to where Mrs. Kilgore was and take her hand or put her arm around her. I can see it now, Mrs. Kilgore at the sink with her back to us—she was a fairly wide woman, and tall too—and little Susan coming up behind her and wrapping her arms around her waist and laying her head over sideways against Mrs. Kilgore's back.

And I started to notice what Susan liked and what she didn't like. She was always trying out different colors of lipstick, some of them real flashy red shades. She liked eye makeups and was real particular about her hair. But when it come to her hands, it was different. Never used nail polish. Cut her fingernails short and straight across. Her hands was clean but rough-looking, like a man's, except for the rings she liked to wear. She was right partial to jewelry, no doubt about that. Nothing that cost too much, but she had lots of beads and pins and earbobs, and they looked good on her.

Susan had learned the things a woman was supposed to know from her Aunt Lenora, who never had a man herself but who wasn't bothered by that in the least. When Susan's mama died giving birth, her daddy wasn't ready to take care of a baby by himself, and he left her with his sister Lenora till Susan was a little older, he said, and then he planned on coming back to get her, which he never did do. He went off down to Florida and started to work around Miami. He'd write letters and sometimes he'd call on the phone, but over the years the letters and the calls fell off, and one day Aunt Lenora told Susan her daddy had had a heart attack and died. Susan said she didn't know how to act when she found that out. Said she knew she was supposed to cry and all, but she'd never laid eyes on the man in person, not that she could remember, and so the fact that he was gone for good now didn't mean too much, even though it was supposed to. It was like the way she was supposed to feel about her mama, who she didn't know the first thing about, since her aunt didn't know her or any of her mama's folks, and her daddy wasn't around to tell about her. One time when he had got a picture of Susan in the mail — she must have been about six or seven — her daddy wrote back and said she'd got her mama's good looks, but that was about it.

So her Aunt Lenora was all Susan had. And to hear Susan tell it, her aunt was sharp as a straight razor. Said she made a living by buying and selling things. I reckon you'd have to call it junk, unless you was trying to sell it to somebody, and then you might call it a antique or a bargain. She had this old barn out behind her house where she kept the things she come across, and she had learned over the years that it don't make much sense to turn nothing down, since you never know what folks will pay a price for. Her aunt had a old truck she drove around the county, and she wasn't above stopping by the side of the road to go through the trash somebody had left piled up there. She believed she could fix or clean up just about anything, and she'd haul home a load of junk—broken lamps and chairs and old rugs and such—nearly every time she went out. Always told Susan that some folks don't have good sense when it comes to throwing things out, and Susan proved that herself by showing me some of the jewelry her aunt pulled out of the garbage. I remember this one necklace made out of what she said was real silver, and it had these green jewels set in it, and when Susan put it on, the way it played off against her hair, it would stop you dead still.

Aunt Lenora knew how to take what nobody else wanted and turn it around so it was worth something. And that's a little like what happened with me.

I ain't saying I was a piece of junk, but inside I was all broke up. And when Susan told me about the time her aunt brought home one of them windows with colored glass like you find in a church—brought it home all in pieces—and about how they spent many a night putting it together, I could see Susan doing that. I could sure see it.

Every now and then Susan got to talking about the folks she cleaned house for, mostly middle-aged women on the other side of town. There was some that she liked, women that treated her good, even called her Mrs. Burt, women that didn't make it seem like they was doing her a favor by letting her scrub out their commode.

But then there was folks like this Mrs. Jarvis, whose husband run Jarvis Department Store in town. The woman stood over Susan while she ironed. Told her she took too long when she went to the bathroom. Made her stop work and serve tea to the garden club women that come by. Called her "my Susan."

And there was a Mrs. Rutherford, wife of a top officer at the bank. She done a inspection every time Susan left the house, and when it come time to pay her, she'd take out a nickel for things she'd have a list of, like streaks on the glasses or dust on the windowsills. She'd go off and leave Susan with a 12-room house to clean, and she'd expect her to baby-sit her two small children too — one of them just starting to walk and into everything, and the other one a whiny, spoiled little boy about four years old who thought Susan was his personal slave. Every time the woman come back home, he cried and run to her, even if he was fine right before then, and he'd be pointing at Susan and saying she was mean and he hated her and so forth. So Mrs. Rutherford would sit Susan down and talk to her while the little boy looked at her with his eyes smiling and his bottom lip pouted out.

I told her to quit the damn jobs, and what's more, I told her I didn't believe that the woman who left my house to go to work was the same one who showed up there, if that was how she acted, letting them women treat her like a dog. It didn't fit with what I knew about her, and I told her that.

She said I didn't understand. "These women, I just shut them out. Get used to them like a bad smell. It's like I throw a switch inside me and they ain't even there."

24

What she told me about shutting folks out was not a big surprise. Sometimes she'd do that with me too. I don't mean she wouldn't talk—we could both get along without talking too much anyhow—but that she'd start to seem like she was far away, in a place where I couldn't get to her. Her eyes would change, and she wouldn't do nothing for a long time, just sit there. I'd let her be. I might put my arms around her or hold her hand, and she might let me, but she was just as likely not to.

And I knew too that her getting like that wasn't really nothing, not up against what come over me from time to time, and which is a main part of this whole story.

But to tell everything, I have to tell about W.D., which stood for Wheelus Dillard, my daddy's name. Me and Susan named our little boy W.D. after my daddy. I wanted to make him W.D., Jr., but she said no, said it was only if his daddy was W.D. that he could be junior. I said all right, so he was W.D., which, I found out, some folks thought was no name for a baby. We'd be out strolling him around and folks would ask what his name was, and when we told them, they might look at us funny. One lady said we ought to be ashamed.

The whole time Susan was expecting, but especially right at the end, I was worried to death, afraid she'd have a accident and lose the baby, but mainly afraid there'd be something wrong with it. I couldn't hardly deal with thinking about that, but I never mentioned it to Susan. I was brought up with all kinds of old superstitions about marking a baby, and I'm not superstitious, but I didn't see no reason to take chances.

And Susan, she had a right hard time of it. When she got sick, sometimes it lasted all day, and then in the last months, when the baby was heavy, she had these backaches that almost killed her. I say that, but I've thought many times that having a baby put such a strain on her body it could have killed her easy, like it did her own mama. She was a strong woman, but she was little, and carrying the baby was hard on her. Her skin got to looking sort of washed-out, and you could tell by looking at her eyes that she wasn't real well.

But she was happy, no doubt about that, and she enjoyed talking about what our baby was going to be like. If it was a girl, it might grow up to be a schoolteacher—she liked that idea—and if it was a boy, maybe he'd own him a factory or a bank, she'd say. She went on with all kinds of stories, making guesses about what the baby would look like when it was born, and when she come to that part, I'd be likely to head off to do a chore in another part of the house, since it made me start to imagine the baby with feet like a pig and a head ballooned up like a jack-o'-lantern.

Before Susan quit work, Mrs. Rutherford used to go on about how she looked. Said you could always look at a woman and tell she was expecting because of how she had that special glow. Of course, Susan was showing before this woman had the first clue, and even then she didn't let Susan ease off on her work, so if she glowed, it was plain old sweat.

One afternoon we was sitting out on the porch, and we seen a storm coming up off to the southwest. The storm cloud put me in mind of them old barns that lean sideways like they're about to fall over. It was real dark and it looked like it might have been fixing to blow around us; I couldn't tell.

We always joked later on about it being a sign from heaven that Susan's water broke right when it started to rain. And it was a wild storm. The rain looked silver at first and then got dark like smoke, and when it hit the tin roof, you would have thought you was back in the weave shop. The wind slammed limbs against the house,

26

and when I come back the next day I seen how the tin on one side of the roof was ripped up and twisted sideways.

And in the middle of all this was when it hit me that I needed to take Susan to the hospital. We had it all worked out. Since we didn't have no car, we planned to get a ride from Mrs. Gasaway, three houses over. She was a spinner on third shift, and she told us to come get her any time, night or day, and she'd drive us up there. I tried calling her, but the line was dead. Lightning started popping all around, and it got more scary-looking outside, but when Susan had a contraction, and with the way she moaned and how her face looked, I knew we couldn't stay there no more. I went and grabbed a blanket off the bed, threw it over Susan and carried her out into the storm, with her yelling at me and beating on me with her fists and calling me stupid, but I was as strong right then as I've ever been in my life, though I'll admit it might not be the smartest thing I've ever done. The rain stung my face and neck and the wind whipped the trees around, but I cut through it without taking a step sideways, and Susan felt light as a pillow in my arms.

When we got to Mrs. Gasaway's house, she looked at me like I was crazy at first, but then she didn't waste no time. Me and Susan got in the back seat of her car, and the woman took off. But then she just drove like she was going to the grocery, even stopped for a red light. I told her to go on. She turned around and flat-out told me to shut up. Said that maybe I didn't know too much about these things, but that she did, and there wasn't no reason to go completely hog wild, and she wasn't about to go racing through town running red lights in a driving rain when you couldn't see five feet in front of your face.

I sat back and didn't say nothing else, just held Susan's hand, and in a few minutes we pulled up to the hospital and Susan and

Mrs. Gasaway went off with a nurse and left me sitting out in the waiting room, soaking wet.

About thirteen hours later W.D. was born. A nurse come out and said I had a fine baby boy. She showed me a card they'd made a footprint on, the foot not much bigger than my thumb, but it looked just right—a normal baby's foot.

And the first time I sat on the edge of the bed beside Susan, with W.D. snuggled up next to her asleep, I leaned down and kissed them both. Right then I raised up all of a sudden and looked around me, like something else was supposed to happen, since I knew it deep down, knew it for a fact, that the world was never meant to be as good as that.

4

Where I live now is in Monroe, a little town about two hours north of Red Oak. I been here for about two years. I started out mostly doing yard work for folks—cutting grass and hedges and raking leaves and cleaning off roofs, but my balance is pretty well shot, and I don't trust myself up on a roof.

They've got a cotton mill here, but it's a lot bigger than the one I used to work in down at Red Oak. I went over there one time and talked to the folks in the weave shop, thinking maybe I could still fix looms, even though I ain't done it in over forty years, but I could tell as soon as I walked out on the floor that I couldn't. I looked at one of them new-type looms, and I didn't even know what I was looking at. I couldn't no more fix one of them things than I could fly a jet plane.

I found me a room in a place above town, a house owned by a man named Pete DeAngelo. Pete's from up around Detroit somewhere, and he used to work in one of the car factories up there, but when he got laid off he found him a job down here, over in the big plant at Doraville. He got him a good deal on a house in Monroe, and he used to drive in to work every day.

His wife's been dead about ten years now, and his children—they had a boy and a girl—they live way off up North, and they got their own families, and they can't get down here to see him.

It's just a little house, and I ain't got but one room barely big enough to turn around in, and me and Pete have to use the same bathroom, but then I don't pay him much rent, so I can't complain.

Pete had to retire from the plant when he hurt his back. Got to where he couldn't hardly walk, much less bend over like he needed to. Then when the doctor operated on him, that made it a whole lot worse, and that's when he had to quit. Says if he had to do it over again, he wouldn't let them cut on him.

Everything he does now, Pete does it straight up, like he's got a broomstick strapped to his back. Walks straight up, sits in a chair straight up, and when he wants to turn his head to look at you, he'll turn his whole body sideways. And most of the time, he's in a lot of pain.

The first day I come to town, I seen a sign out in a yard saying there was a room to rent. I knocked on the door and this stiff-necked man opened it and said, "Yeah?"

I said, "I seen your sign out yonder. That looks like about what I can handle."

The man looked at me real hard. "Oh yeah? What's it say?"

"Twenty-five dollars a week."

He shook his whole body back and forth, like his head wouldn't move. Then he said it was a old sign he should have already taken down. Said it was more than what the sign said.

"Well," I asked him, "how much you want?"

He didn't answer me right off. Frowned at me like he thought I was simpleminded or something, and then he said he wasn't even sure he wanted to rent the room anymore.

"Well," I said. I knew what he was telling me, seeing as how I *wasn't* simpleminded, and I knew I'd have to find me someplace else, and so before I left I asked him if he had any idea where I could find me a room for about the price he had out there on his sign.

He said, "I can't help you there, buddy."

He shut the door real quick, and I went on down the street and then walked through a good part of the town, carrying my suitcase, looking to see if there was any other places to rent cheap, but I didn't see none. And then by accident, since I didn't have no idea where I was, I come past the man's house again and for some reason he opened his front door and yelled at me.

"Hey, you."

"Yes sir?" I said.

"Thirty-five a week," he said, "bottom price. Pay in advance."

I reckon it was my turn then, and I took a good look at him, trying to figure whether or not he was a man I wanted to live in the same house with, but I didn't think about it too long. Once you've spent a while in the state prison, you get over being too picky, and I said, "Fine by me," and walked up and give him the thirty-five dollars, and we went on from there.

The whole time I've lived in Monroe, I've been in the habit of taking me a walk every day, even when I'm tired from working. At first I'd always walk up Broad Street and through town, and then on out the highway a piece. Out there a good ways there's this nursing home where I'd always turn around and start back, but I'd generally sit there and rest a little bit first. It wasn't too long after I had moved here and started taking my walks that I noticed how high the grass was getting at that nursing home, and I went in and asked did they want somebody to cut it. They said the man that usually took care of it was out sick, and so I done it for them, and after that they put me on part-time out there, and so now I cut the grass and I work there as a janitor pretty regular too.

Pete's got him a car, a old white '59 Chevy, one of them models with the sharp sideways fins on it. He's got it sitting down low, and he keeps it clean and waxed up. Got him one of them plastic religious statues on the dashboard. He's out in the yard with the hood up on that car all the time, but he can't hardly bend over to work on it, even though he'll still try. It seems to me one reason he talks so much is that there ain't much work he *can* do, his back being like it is. He's been used to having a job all his life, and now he mostly sits at home, feeling like he's supposed to be somewhere else doing something. Let somebody come to the door or call him on the phone and he'll talk them into next week.

At first, I thought Pete was just being charitable when he offered to carry me to work, and then later on I seen that he wasn't doing it just for me. He likes to drive, and then too he wanted to get in on the job, so he'd have something to occupy him. Of course, with his back like it is there ain't much yard work he can do. He did try at first; got down on his knees, but his back still hurt him too much for him to stay there very long.

For a while he sort of took on the role of overseer, even though I was the only one getting paid. Before I cut the grass, we'd walk across the place, looking for sticks and rocks and such as that, things that might get caught in the lawnmower. He couldn't bend down to get them himself, but he'd point them out to me, so I could pick them up. And then when I started to mow, sometimes he'd stand at the edge of the place I was cutting, and every now and then he'd try to shout over the noise of the mower, trying to tell me something. He'd point out a spot I missed, or he'd yell at me to cut the yard crossways instead of up and down, or he'd yell at me to hurry up because he thought it was going to rain.

These days he mostly just gives me a ride, since I do mostly janitor work there now, and Pete don't care much for going inside the nursing home. He's got a good heart, and it really gets him down to go inside and to see what a fix so many of the folks are in. I'd be lying if I said it didn't get me down too.

5

I remember one day when I was playing with W.D., when I started teasing him and I let it get out of hand. He was about three years old then. We'd been rolling a ball across the floor, back and forth, and then one time I slipped it up under my shirt and played like it was lost. He started looking for it, and he couldn't figure it out, and then after a while he got upset and started to cry. Susan had the ironing board set up in the same room, and she seen what I had done, and at first she smiled at it, but then when W.D. thought his ball was lost and started to cry, she stopped ironing and looked at me and cocked her head sideways.

Now if anybody was to hurt W.D., any way at all, they'd answer to me. Sometimes I'd get so worried about him, it wasn't natural. I used to stand over his bed and watch him sleep, making sure he was still breathing.

But that day, instead of saying I was sorry and handing the ball back, I tried to cover it up by acting like I was trying to teach W.D. a lesson. Instead of owning up to playing a little trick that turned mean, I ended up telling Susan a lie about how I was letting the baby see that you can't get everything you want all the time.

She didn't pay me the least bit of attention. She said, "Ellis Burt, you give that baby his ball back right this minute."

I took the ball out of my shirt—a hard rubber ball—and I flipped it sideways at W.D. At least I meant to flip it, but I got too much of my arm into it, and I guess you could say I slung it, like a child might have done, and it hit him slap on his left eye, and he fell back howling.

Susan grabbed him up and took him into the kitchen and put a cold washrag on his eye. And I followed them in there, said I was sorry and I didn't mean to do that, but W.D. was screaming and Susan had cut me dead, and if I reached out to try to touch W.D.'s face, she'd twist him away so I couldn't reach him, and if I tried to put my arm around her, she swung a mean elbow at me. I stepped back and watched her tend to his eye.

I had learned a long time ago that you can almost never talk yourself out of a situation. On the other hand, if you try it, you can get yourself in a whole lot more trouble real easy. And so I finally went on about my business like always, except I done some things I didn't usually do. Without saying anything about it, I washed the supper dishes, and when it come time to go to sleep, I brought Susan a big glass of ice water to put by the bed. She always wanted one, since she got thirsty in the night, and when we first got married I done it for her, but I had stopped. And then the next day I brought home a plastic ball and bat for W.D., and after a while things got back to normal.

I thought about it a lot after that—how easy one thing had led to another, and how I'd ended up hurting W.D. when that was the last thing in the world I wanted to do.

And while I was thinking about what I'd done, I couldn't help remembering the time my mama done something she never meant to, a long time ago—something that hurt me bad, something she never had the least idea she was going to do, even though when she got going she put everything she had into it.

Neither Mama or Daddy ever touched whiskey, except to use as medicine, like when they made up some of what they called ginger tea to burn off a cold or the flu. They'd take some ginger root and grind it up real good and boil it and then put whiskey in it and drink it themselves or make us drink it. It was the worst tasting stuff in the world, but it would sweat the fire out of you, sweat you plumb to death. Other than that, they didn't touch liquor. Signed a oath down at the church. My daddy's brother, Uncle Mack, he was bad to use whiskey, but that's another story.

Mama kept this jar of clear whiskey stuck down behind some cans in the pantry, kept it there just to use for medicine. Makes me wonder now where they come up with it, whether they bought it off of Uncle Mack. That would have been a sight—Mama in a whiskey deal with Uncle Mack. But it wasn't no store-bought stuff; it was shine, clear as spring water.

It was after Daddy died, and things was real hard. One evening when Mama and me had come in from the field and I'd gone off down by the creek with the dog for a while, I come back home and I seen Mama hadn't cooked nothing. She had the jar of whiskey setting right out on the table, and a glass half full of it in front of her. I could tell she was drunk; I'd seen that look plenty, on Uncle Mack and his friends, when they'd come around the house. It has to do with the eyes—how they look sort of easy and wild at the same time.

Mama had that look, and she was slid down in the chair, her feet sticking way out. She just waved at me when I walked up, like it was the most natural thing in the world for her to be sitting there blowed away.

I said, "Mama, are you all right?"

She smiled at me, and her face didn't seem to quite fit her, like her mouth was on crooked somehow, and she said, "I had a toothache, and I pulled this stuff out to give me a little relief, and I reckon it's give me too much. But I'm going to get up and get us some supper now, hon. You go on and rinch your hands off."

I went out to the well and drew some water, but when I come back she hadn't moved, and it looked like she'd poured more whiskey in the glass. I could see then that she wasn't up to doing nothing, and I said for her to stay right where she was at, and I'd cook us up something. She nodded and took a drink. I boiled some Irish potatoes and heated up a mess of peas and some cornbread that was left over from the night before and set us out some pepper sauce and sweet cooked tomatoes for the peas, and all the while Mama didn't say nothing, which was odd, since she was always the one in the family that didn't mind talking. Used to get right peeved at me and Daddy for how we could sit at the table a whole meal and not say a word and feel easy with it. I don't mean she was the kind to rattle on about nothing, but she liked to talk a right smart and to have somebody to talk to.

And so when she drunk all that whiskey and got quiet, it felt like something was bad wrong. And then she wouldn't eat nothing, wouldn't touch a bite, and there was some streak o'lean still left in the pork fat she'd used for cooking the peas the night before, and she always loved a good piece of streak o'lean, but she didn't even look at it, just kept on drinking. Told me it looked good and thanked me for heating it up, but said she didn't care for nothing.

I ate and put things away, and just as I was finishing, Mama stood up and started off down the hall, but by then she was knee-walking, and she swung sideways into the room where I always slept and braced herself against the wall and made a loud groan. I grabbed hold of her so she wouldn't fall and I helped her over to my cot and made her lay down there, and the minute she hit the cot she was gone, like she'd been hit in the head with a two-by-four. Had her mouth wide open, and she made a kind of snoring, gur-gling noise. She always snored a little when she slept anyhow, and I used to tease her about it, used to tell her it sounded like she had a comb and wax paper at the back of her throat, the way she made that high, wheezy sound. But this here was a different noise—deep and like she was almost choking. I arranged her on the cot, pulled her feet over straight, got the pillow up under her head good and threw the sheet up over her, and then I went across the hall and got in her bed and went to sleep.

Middle of the night I heard her knocking around, fumbling for the slop jar, and then I heard her relieve herself in it and felt her crawl into the bed with me and right off, start snoring again.

I come up out of the black of sleep hearing a whisper, more like a moan; it said "Dubby," which was Mama's pet name for my daddy, W.D. It was still pure dark, and Mama had slid over and locked herself onto my body, had hold of me from the side, with both legs wrapped around my left leg, her chest pinning my left arm down, her arms pulling me towards her. Now Mama was as strong as most men, worked all day long out in the field—her arms hard with muscles, her whole body hard and soft at the same time—and right then she had gripped the back of my neck and put her face up to mine. She smelled like night-breath and sweat and corn liquor, and I could smell her hair, and there was woodsmoke in it. Lord, I can smell it now.

I was thirteen years old, and this was right when I'd started to be ashamed about looking at her the wrong way sometimes, like when she was just wearing a slip. It like to drove me wild, just the way her body might shift a little when she bent down or the way she might pull her dress part way up her leg to rub some cream on her thigh, not paying me the least bit of mind, since she had always done such things, and as far as she knew, I was the same baby boy I'd always been, but I was thirteen then, and not a baby boy, and what part of a man I'd become was pretty much out of control.

But not so out of control that I wanted my own mama rubbing her body on mine. I said real soft, and then loud, "Mama," but she was dreaming and drunk at the same time, and she didn't hear nothing.

"Mama," I shouted, "Mama. I ain't Dubby. I ain't Daddy. I'm me, I'm Ellis." But didn't nothing get through, and she had started to move on my leg, slid up and moved hard against my thighbone, and was trying to roll over on top of me.

Like I said, Mama was lots stronger than me. And when she come at me like that, my right arm was asleep from the way I'd been laying on it, and for a bit there I couldn't raise it. She had me pinned, had got leverage against me, my arm was numb, and she was trying to kiss me on the mouth. I twisted my head way back and to the side, and that's when she kissed me on the ear, and that done it. I come straight up off the bed and knocked Mama off onto the floor, and headed for the door, but it was dark as a lake bottom in there, and I was in her room where I was not used to moving around at night, and I run slap into the wall, and it felt like some-body had shot black pepper up my nose into my brain.

I got on up and went out, went over to my cot and laid down, and right then didn't think too much about Mama being all over me like that, since my nose was killing me. I just laid down and held a cloth over it and went back to sleep.

And then I woke up to Mama standing over me having a fit, wanting to know about the blood. I had blood all down the front of my shirt, and where I'd laid back the blood had run out of my nose and streaked past both eyes, so I had a kind of blood mask on. My nose had swole up like a new potato, and I couldn't breathe out of it. It's crooked to this day, and I breathe out of the left side better than the right.

But that morning when I looked in my mama's eyes, I seen she didn't have no recollection at all about what happened the night before. And unless it come to her later on in some other dream, my mama never knew how she'd laid her sweet body down on her own son and called him a dead man's name, put her hot skin on his and moved the way a woman does, kissed him with her tongue in his ear. And she surely never knew how much he wanted to close his eyes and let go, and how it hurt him inside and made him sick even to think about doing that—raising up to meet her hands and her mouth—and how it kept on coming back to him, even though he didn't want it to, and how he'd pray to Jesus, and how it would come to him in the middle of his prayer—that there must be some things even Jesus could never forgive you for.

The only work Uncle Mack ever had was making whiskey, and even then he didn't want to be the one to run the still, wanted somebody else to do that, since it was hard work. Mama said he was the sorriest excuse for a man she'd ever seen. Said he'd have let somebody else chew his food for him if they'd have made him a serious offer.

When Daddy died, Uncle Mack come around right at first and whimpered and whined, but he never raised a hand to help us out, and after that we didn't hardly ever see him. Then, when he found out the Cutts family was helping us out, he said Daddy never would have wanted his widow taking charity from niggers. Didn't say this directly to Mama though. He sat down at Hodges Store and run his mouth about it. There was a regular group there — men that would sit around most of every day drinking whiskey, smoking cigarettes, playing cards, and talking about politics, which for them meant one thing — what they called the nigger problem. Whatever come up, they'd work it around to niggers. You let us go a spell without rain, they'd find a way to blame it on the niggers, and then they'd get off on why God made niggers in the first place.

My daddy wasn't no agitator — far from it. He didn't think no different from most folks back then, black or white — thought folks ought to pretty much stay with their own kind, and that you got to a point where mixing in just wasn't natural. And even though he couldn't read it, he knew what the Bible said about Noah and Ham and so forth — verses that the preacher said was supposed to account for why black folks was in such a fix. But Daddy said he didn't believe black folks had a real strong itch to be around white folks nohow. They just wanted to be treated right, that was all.

When Uncle Mack come around drinking and spouting off his nigger talk, Daddy didn't ever say much. He'd sit there and be quiet, or he'd bring up something else. I never heard him come back at him but one time, and then he sort of went at him sideways.

Uncle Mack was talking at me, giving me the lowdown, the way he liked to do. "Now, Ellis," he said, "don't you know a nigger ain't nothing but a monkey with clothes on? I mean, you take a good look at them. Get yourself a picture of a monkey and hold it up next to a nigger. Got the same lips, same hair, same skin. Take any black nigger. You take that old Cutts nigger down yonder."

I seen my daddy look up.

Uncle Mack laughed out loud, and he said, "He's so black he can't find hisself in the dark. Ain't but half a step from swinging in the trees like one of them baboons. Look at them arms and listen how he talks. Them monkey lips can't say no big words, and they ain't supposed to. God never meant a nigger or a monkey neither one to talk. You listen to them over there on a Saturday night—listen to any bunch of niggers on a Saturday night—and they'll be whooping and howling and carrying on, and that's when you can see it, the gospel truth. Monkeys straight out of the jungle."

All the while he was talking, Uncle Mack was swigging on a jar of corn liquor, and he was getting right up in my face, breathing it at me.

Now my daddy was a pleasant enough man, but like I said before, he was not what you would call real sociable, and if you had asked him who his best friend was, I don't believe he'd have come up with a name, unless he said my mama. But I could have told you. Leaving Mama out of it, my daddy's best friend was Otis Cutts, whose farm was right next to ours on Mr. Stillwell's land.

My daddy was a halfcropper. We didn't own nothing—not the house or the land or the mule or the plow. All this was Mr. Stillwell's. We done all the work and give Mr. Stillwell half the cotton, the cottonseed, the corn, and whatever else we might have raised. On top of this, he'd have loaned us some rations money to live on, and he might have advanced us some fertilizer, and so when we sold the crop we'd pay him back with interest.

But Otis and Essie Mae Cutts, they weren't no straight share-croppers. They worked on thirds and fourths—give Mr. Stillwell a third of their cotton and a fourth of their corn. They didn't own the house or the land neither, but they had their own mule and plow, and they didn't owe so much for rations since they had three milk cows, and they'd sell some of the milk.

And when Otis seen we needed help, he helped us out, and this was even before my daddy died. So Uncle Mack's carrying on about help from niggers didn't mean nothing to me and mama. Daddy didn't want to take charity from nobody, but he'd have taken it from Otis before he took it from anybody else.

I remember how Daddy leaned over and let his elbow rest on his knee, and then without looking at his brother he said, "You know, Mack, what I been wondering is, since you been such a dumb-ass all your life, how you got to be such a expert on everything now."

Uncle Mack whirled on him. He had the jar in his right hand, but he set it down real careful. "What's that?"

Daddy looked straight at him then. "What I mean is, how did you get so all-fired smart? Talking to them other geniuses down at the store?"

Uncle Mack said, "You want me to kick your ass right here in front of your family? Don't think I won't do it, buddy boy."

To this day, I still wish my daddy had took him up on it. Daddy would have laid him out. He was all muscle and bone, and Uncle Mack was a sloppy mess of boozed-up ham fat.

Uncle Mack stood up and walked toward him. Daddy just looked at him, didn't stand up, didn't move. He said, "It's flat piti-ful, that's what it is. Come in here talking like you know the *first* damn thing." Daddy opened his mouth like he was going to go on, but then he sat back and looked away and threw up a hand and let it drop.

Uncle Mack reached over and got his jar, and when he raised up, he kicked the chair he'd been sitting in, so it slammed against the wall and fell over, and then he turned around and hawked up and spit on the floor, right there in front of my daddy, and then stomped out the door.

When he was gone, Mama got a rag and she was going to wipe up the spit, but Daddy took the rag away from her and told her he'd get it, and he did. And that was when I heard him say to Mama, real low, like he didn't want me to hear him, "Otis Cutts ain't no monkey."

After my daddy died I had to stay home most of the time and work, just so we could scratch out a living on the place, which Mr. Stillwell doubted we could do. At first, he had it in mind to turn Mama and me out, but like I said, Otis and his folks helped us.

I did still go to school as regular as I could. It broke my mama's heart when I had to start missing out so much. Her and Daddy was both big on school, and they was set on me getting educated and having a better life than them.

Yellow Shoals was a lot smaller than Ricksville, but since Mr. Stillwell's children went there, it had a better school. Mr. Stillwell threw his weight around and got a new building built, got new books every so often, and got the best teachers he could find. The school looked like it was out of a picture book—red brick, with a playground beside it and a flagpole in front. The pages of most of the books was stiff and the edges clean. I'd always have new books since I was in Alice's grade and Mr. Stillwell seen to it that she didn't use no old books.

We had a good teacher too. Mrs. Partain was a widow whose husband had been a cotton farmer. They'd had them a place about fifty miles south, and they was right well off at one time, or at least people said so—she never talked about it, said it wasn't good manners to talk about yourself that way, especially when it had to do with money.

I can see Mrs. Partain like it was yesterday. She had gray hair, and she pulled it back into a tight bun. By the time most children was in the fifth grade they was already as tall as her, but let me tell you, that was one big woman to be so little. She could make you do what she wanted without laying a finger on you. I seen her pop a student on the behind every now and then, but she didn't need to give no big whippings, like I heard they had over in Ricksville every day. Most times, Mrs. Partain could just look at you and that would do it. That woman could stare a hole through a jailhouse wall. And she'd know your folks too, and she'd talk to them regular about you, and so if any whipping had to be done, they'd be the ones to do it.

Now Mrs. Partain, she had this idea that country folks ought to learn everything city folks did, and so she taught us lots of history, like about Rome and so forth. And she made us get up and recite things we'd had to memorize. She'd make us stand just right, hold our hands right. She'd make us talk out so everybody could hear us.

But then she made us do other things that you didn't have in most schools, I reckon. She taught us how to act if you went to somebody's house—how to introduce yourself, when to talk and when not to. She even taught us how to sit and how to hold a tea-cup, and that was a sight. Didn't everybody always wear shoes to school, and there we'd be, sitting on this sofa she had brung in, sitting up there all proper with both bare feet flat on the floor and balancing a teacup in our hands.

And she'd separate the boys and girls and she'd talk to us about how to act towards each other later on when we started courting. She told us what girls liked and what they wanted to hear, told us how they expected to be treated, and she done the same thing about us with the girls. One time she got in trouble because she put the boys and girls together and proceeded to teach us the proper way to act at a dance—how to ask for a dance, where to put your hands, what to do when you started to sweat, what to say when the dance was over, and so forth. Everybody around there was mostly Baptists and they seen dancing as a sin, but Mrs. Partain herself was Episcopalian, and she didn't see it as nothing but dancing. For a while there they planned to throw her out over teaching dancing, but she apologized, and they never did.

I didn't have no special feeling towards Alice Stillwell. Like I said, she treated me nice, but that was all. That day when Mrs. Partain taught us how to act at a dance, she paired us off. She done it partly by height so we wouldn't look silly. She didn't want a real tall girl with a short boy; the other way around didn't matter. Me and Alice ended up dancing together.

Now I'd touched girls before—shoot, I'd wrestled them—but this was different. The way Mrs. Partain had it set up, you had to think about every little touch you made. Like when you come up to the girl, she had to put out her hand in a certain way, and you had to take it a certain way. You thought about all that before you touched her, and so just the littlest touch got real important, and that changed everything, put a charge in it that I understood later on, but one that puzzled me right then.

There was this way you had to put your hand across the girl's back—real soft but firm at the same time, and you wasn't supposed to move it around back there. That was bad manners. You had to lay it there just right. And then you had to look at her some while y'all danced, and you had to do that real careful too. You couldn't look away the whole time, but you had to do it a little bit, otherwise you'd be staring. And when you did look her in the eyes you had to hold your eyes just right—couldn't look hard, couldn't squint neither, or wink. You had to look at her straight, with a steady and pleasant look, like it was the most natural thing in the world. One thing I learned back then was that dancing by the rules would wear you slap out.

The day after me and Alice danced with each other, we was by ourselves out in the hall for a minute, and I started to feel uneasy and it seemed like she did too, and I blurted out something I never would have said otherwise. It just popped out of my mouth. I said, "I'd give a dollar to see that special room in y'all's house that has all them war things."

"What?" she said.

"I said I'd like to see that room y'all got—you know, with them uniforms and such all laid out. Your great-granddaddy's stuff, all his things from the War Between the States."

"We don't have a room like that," she said.

I thought she was teasing me now, since everybody knew about that room. I'd heard lots of folks talk about it, and besides, Alice had brung in that tintype of her great-granddaddy and that famous general and showed it off, and so when I said what I said back to her, I reckon I made it sound kind of smart-alecky.

"Y'all *don't* have no fancy room with war stuff all laid out?"

She asked me where I'd got such a crazy idea. Said upstairs in her daddy's office there was a Confederate hat and coat hung on the wall, and in one drawer of his desk he had some things, like letters and pictures and orders, and he had a old pistol in there. She wanted to know where I got the idea they had a special room.

I could see she was serious, and now I felt like a fool, but I didn't want her to think I'd just made it up. Like I said, I'd heard lots of folks talk about it, and that's what I told her, and I reckon the way I said it made her see that some folks thought of it as a kind of joke, because she got real mad at me then. She said people said things about her family all the time. Said folks made up things that was plumb crazy or just plain mean. She stomped back into the room and sat down and wouldn't talk to me or look at me for the rest of the day.

I was walking home that afternoon when Mr. Stillwell pulled up right beside me in his car, and Alice rolled down her window and said, "Get in."

I looked over at Mr. Stillwell's red face, and I said "Naw, Alice, I can't . . ."

Mr. Stillwell leaned over and across his daughter, and he spit out the words "Get in."

I got in, and we rode to their house fast, with nobody saying a word, and when we got out of the car Mr. Stillwell come over and grabbed me by a strap on my overalls and started dragging me up the steps, jerking at the strap like I was a mule. I was doing the best I could to keep up with him, but he knew which way he was going and I didn't, and so I'd lose a step and he'd jerk on the strap. He drug me from room to room, drug me all over the house, upstairs and downstairs, cussing at me under his breath. I don't know if Alice could hear it or not, but I turned back to look at her one time and her face looked like she was about to cry. He'd throw open a door and sling me into a room, then jerk me back out of it and drag me down the hall, and when it was all done, he pulled me out to the back steps and give me a shove, and I don't think he meant to throw me down, but I tripped and cut my knee on the edge of one of the steps.

I went on to the bottom and then looked back, and Alice was crying now, and Mr. Stillwell said, "Burt, you ever talk smart to my daughter again, I'll skin you alive. You understand?"

I nodded.

He come halfway down the steps. "You understand me?"

"Yes sir," I said.

They went back into the house and I walked home, and I never said a word to Mama or Daddy about what happened, since I thought they would get mad at Mr. Stillwell and something bad might come of it.

The next day at school I seen Alice, and she said she was sorry. Said she never meant for that to happen, never even wanted me to get in the car. She was sorry she'd ever told him what I'd said. I believed it, since I knew Alice pretty good from being with her at school, and she wouldn't ever treat nobody else like that.

Time went on, and me and her got to be better friends, and not too long after all this she come to school about to bust. At recess she pulled me off to the side and she told me her daddy had gone and fixed him up a room like the one I'd told her everybody already thought they had. He'd took a bedroom upstairs and painted it and laid everything out—made him a war museum after all.

And so it was our little secret—mine and Alice's, though I reckon Mr. Stillwell was in on it too—how the lie that folks had made up and told over and over had finally turned itself into the truth.

6

All her life, Susan's Aunt Lenora had told her not to trust nobody, especially people that wanted to help her, and especially men. That's how come she acted the way she did when I pulled the Waycross boys off her. And she wasn't but nineteen at the time. Her aunt had been dead for two years then, almost as long as it had took the cancer to kill her. After that, Susan supported herself working as a housecleaner. When we was first married, she told me she'd worked some at cleaning houses, but she didn't let on she'd been doing it full time to make a living. Why not, I don't know, except that it could take her a long time to open up about personal things.

After her aunt died, Susan had to move out of the house. And then she lived in a rented room, sharing a bathroom and kitchen with a family of four that she almost never talked to. The house was a short walk from the fairgrounds, and that was why she was at the fair that day, and why we met each other. She could see the fair from her window, and she'd walked over there.

And going to the fair was something she'd always done with her Aunt Lenora, and so it reminded her of good times when she went there. She told me that right at first her aunt used to come back to her in her dreams, and it would be like she was really alive again. Susan told herself she was dreaming—she knew it—but even then, the dream made her believe it was real, and when she'd wake up, it was like her aunt had died all over again.

And Susan fixed up her rented room the way she knew her aunt would have liked it. She picked bunches of wildflowers and put them all over the room, like her aunt had always done, and she opened up the windows and raised the blinds, so there was breezes and lots of light, the way her aunt liked it.

Aunt Lenora liked to put flowers in her own hair and in Susan's. The morning we got married Susan walked out and found her a flower she said was a wild shamrock, and she had that flower in her hair when she married me. It was like a little violet. She said her aunt told her one time that it stood for good luck in your marriage.

W.D. was two years old before one of my spells hit me again, and he was with me when it happened. Susan had gone off to the store, and W.D. and me was out in the yard, and all of a sudden I was breathing like I'd run a mile as fast as I could, my heart going like that too, my stomach twisted up like a rope, the sky going around and the trees going around.

Renfroe was out in his yard cutting the grass, and Bull Watson was on his porch, and they seen me fall down, and Renfroe run over there shouting to his wife Alma that I'd done had a heart attack. I knew it wasn't no heart attack, and I managed to tell him so, and he wanted to know what the hell it was, but I just laid back on the grass and shook my head, and just like that it went away.

I laid there looking at the sky, and W.D.'s little face come down over me, his eyes real wide, and he was crying, and I grabbed hold of him and hugged him, and when Susan come home, I told her it wasn't nothing, not really, and that I had probably just got dizzy from working too hard, and she acted like she believed me.

Over the years I went to a few doctors about my spells. They always thought I might have been a epileptic, but then they'd test me and find out I wasn't.

49

When a spell hit me, I'd get a sick feeling all over, kind of like a shock, like it shot through me and speeded everything up, so my heart beat real fast, and I couldn't hardly catch my breath. But it was more than that: when a spell hit me, it was like I'd lost my mind.

It was getting to where I knew I was going to have to do something about it. One day I was smoking a cigarette outside on my break when I heard these two weavers shouting back and forth, both of them deaf as a rubber boot, talking about the revival being held that week at a little church down below town. I wasn't trying to listen, but I didn't have no choice. One of them was saying that his sister went down there and got healed.

"Gospel truth," he said. "She went down there and this preacher laid hands on her, and them pains she'd been having in her head and her neck? They disappeared, just like that."

He said she come back to the house so full of the spirit couldn't nobody stand her. The other man said he was going down there after work and see could he get some help for his stomach.

It was the hottest day of the summer, tar bubbling up on the paved roads, and the air so heavy it felt like you had to push your way through it. You couldn't hardly stand it in the mill. Five minutes into my shift I was sopping wet, sweat dripping off me when I bent over a loom. I was working first shift at the time. Susan and me had made an agreement that if I hadn't got home by the middle of the afternoon, that meant I was working overtime — which I always tried to do — and so she didn't have to worry, since she knew I'd be home when second shift ended, after ten o'clock. The day when I heard them weavers talking about the revival, it was only three days after I had fell out at work, right there in the weave shop. Folks thought the heat had got to me, and they sat me in front of one of them big fans and give me a glass of ice water. I hadn't never had a spell at work before, and it worried me. I knew I couldn't start falling out at work or I'd be out of a job.

And so at the end of my shift I hung around down in the machine shop, like I had business down there, which I sometimes did, and I moved around the mill talking with folks here and there, like I was just on a break and had stopped by to see them. I got to feeling like a regular politician, moving around like that, pretending to be at work. I spent some time in the spinning room, and over by the slubbers, and talking to some doffers in the card room, all the while hiding out. I stayed away from the weave shop, and then when it got late enough I started out walking.

The church was about two miles south of the mill, but if I cut through the black section I could save a half mile or so, maybe more. Red Oak had two black sections, two patches of shotgun houses and dirt roads—one of them called Cozy Town and the other one just Davis Street. I turned off through Cozy Town, since it was in the crook of the highway, and it didn't make no sense to walk that curve when I could cut straight across.

I'd spent some time in Cozy Town and on Davis Street both—not much—but I'd had business in there. And it wasn't nothing for a white man to walk through either place, not back then, if he was just walking through and not looking to cause no trouble. That evening there was already some lights on, folks out on their porches and in the street, children running around. I remember some of them trying to catch lightning bugs and how they kicked up red dust from the street. Smells of supper drifted out of the houses—chicken and barbecue and fried fish and cornbread and hushpuppies. Every now and then somebody nodded at me, and I nodded back.

I come up on a old woman out sweeping her yard with a dogwood brush broom. The dirt yard was set off from the street by a square border of tires cut in half and whitewashed, and she had swept that yard as clean and flat as a pine board. The old woman straightened up from her sweeping when I come by and said, "How you this evening?"

"Heat's about got me," I said. "How you?"

She hobbled over and leaned on her brush broom, and I seen she didn't have a tooth in her head. "Well, you know, some days I ain't fit to kill. This old arthritis. Hot day like this ain't too bad, but now the cold weather? It just freeze up on me, make it hard to even get out the bed. You lay in the house and don't do nothing all day. Feel like your bones is about to break clean in two. Where you going?"

When I told her I was headed over to Mt. Zion to the revival, she said, "Child, they say that white man healing and carrying on like nobody business."

She stood there then with her chin stuck out and her head sort of cocked to one side, like it was my turn to talk and hers to listen.

I told her I reckoned I'd better be getting on, and she said, "Well," and she waved me off on down the road with her hand, like she was slapping at a horsefly, and she turned away real quick and went back to sweeping.

The service had done started when I got there. The back door was open and I stood and waited with two other folks while somebody finished praying, and then I went inside and squeezed in on the back row next to this fat woman and some others who looked like they might be some of her family. She looked at me like I was crazy when I started to try to wedge myself in there, but I was tired from working all day and from walking and I wasn't about to stand up no more if I could help it.

The preacher whose church it was, a Reverend Lumpkin, welcomed everybody, introduced Brother James Oakley, the revival preacher, and then led us in a hymn. We stood up and sung "What a Friend We Have in Jesus," and when we went to sit down again the force of all them wide folks hitting the bench at once shot sideways and squashed me against the arm of the pew, and I got up and walked down the left aisle and found me a place on the second row.

Sitting up that close, I could see Brother Oakley real good. Even in that heat, he was wearing a heavy blue suit, and he never took his coat off all night, and I could see where he'd sweated clean through it even before he started. When he got to preaching, he took off real slow, talked in a quiet voice, so the folks in the back probably had to strain to hear him, but then he picked it up. He didn't waste no time on thank yous or hellos or nothing like that. He went straight to work, told three Bible stories—one about how Jesus prayed for mercy in the garden; one about how this woman reached out and touched Jesus and got healed, even though Jesus didn't know who touched him; and one about how Jesus cast the demons out of a man called Legion.

He stopped right then and looked at us, let his eyes go across the whole room, and you couldn't hear nothing but a pew creaking under somebody's weight, and then a dog barked twice far off, and you could hear it through the open windows, and then it was dead quiet.

Brother Oakley took out his handkerchief from his inside coat pocket and wiped his face and put it back and he reached down and picked up his Bible again. He looked up at us then and he smiled, and he said, "I'm happy to see all of you here this evening. So happy to see these families."

He stepped back from the pulpit then and took a deep breath and looked down, and when he looked up he said, "Three stories from the gospel, and when you look at them, this is what you have: you've got the Redeemer himself asking for mercy, sweating blood, down on his knees, asking his own father, the Lord God Almighty, to let him be. But he won't. And you've got this: you've got devils that have made their nest in a man, devils that start to cry and grieve when holiness comes toward them, and they howl out to Jesus, asking for mercy, and he listens to them, listens to the demons—understand what I'm telling you—and he gives them what they asked for."

Brother Oakley stood there with his palms raised up and a frown on his face, and then he let his arms drop, and he walked down out of the pulpit, and he spoke real low, and he said, "And between the voice of the Savior and the voice of the devils, both asking for mercy, you have the silence of the woman who was bleeding to death and who came forth and just put out her hand without a word.

"This what I've come to ask you tonight, my friends: where do *you* belong?

"And if you don't know, if you don't know already, I'll tell you." He was whispering again now. "You are right there with that silent woman—between Christ and the demons, and you need to reach out your hand. You need to reach your hand out to Jesus."

And while Brother Oakley was still preaching, a couple rose and a little boy—must have been about five—stood up with them, and they each one held one of his hands and they walked to the front of the church, and Brother Oakley broke off and said, "Praise God."

And he stepped down off the platform then, and he leaned over and whispered to the couple and they whispered back to him, and he squatted down and said something to the boy, who looked up at his mama like he didn't know what to do. His mama nodded and the boy nodded then, and the preacher stood back up and he spoke to the congregation.

He told us their names was Thelma and Harris Fambrough, and Roy, their son, who'd had rheumatic fever a while back and who was deaf now. He asked us to pray for the boy, and then he turned to the woman at the piano and nodded to her, and she started to play "Wherever He Leads I'll Go." She played it real soft, and she had gone through the first verse of it when Brother Oakley picked up the boy and went and sat down on the platform and asked the mama and daddy to sit on either side of him while he held the boy on his lap. He didn't put on a big show. The way he laid hands on this boy to heal him was the way a mama might take a child on her lap who has bumped his head real bad. She holds him and rocks him and says to him that he's going to be all right, and she strokes his head and kisses his hair. Brother Oakley done all that, and then all of a sudden he just raised his right hand and said, "Lord, in the name of Jesus, we ask your healing mercy on this child. Amen."

Then he put his hand down and laid it soft on the boy's head, and then passed him over into his mother's arms. The boy's mama whispered something to the boy, turned him away from her and whispered again, and then she looked at the preacher, and her face broke open, and she shook her head no.

Brother Oakley said something to her that I couldn't hear, and then he led the couple back to their seat and returned to the pulpit. "Young brother and sister," he said, "I can only speak to you tonight out of the Scriptures, which promise that the mercy of the Lord is everlasting, that his truth endures, and that he has promised you that he will not leave you alone, but he will come to you in the spirit."

The service went on, but as for me, I stayed where I was at, never stepped forward, though I seen a man with a bad arm go up and after a quiet prayer start to wave it all around, and I heard a woman with a stutter come back down the aisle talking like she belonged on the radio.

From where I was sitting, I could see that little deaf boy and his folks, and I watched them when we sung the last hymn. The daddy's face was all locked up, and the mama held the hymnbook and just looked at it, and the little boy sat in the crook of his daddy's right arm and looked straight back at me. He rolled his eyes and stuck his tongue out sideways, making the kind of silly face a child will, and then he laughed—laughed while his daddy held him—and something about that child's look has stayed with me all my life, like it was a picture I carried in my billfold.

I walked back home the same way I come, through Cozy Town. It was a full moon, and the sky was blue-black over the pines, and when I hit the main road that cut through Cozy Town I could see the houses outlined against the sky. Wasn't nobody out in the street now. I could hear talking coming from the houses; I heard some music here and there, somebody playing a guitar out on their front porch. Dogs barked at me, but didn't none of them chase me. And walking past the houses, I got that feeling I used to have when I was a boy, when I used to look at the houses of folks I didn't know, see a lamp in their window, and it would bother me and puzzle me that their lives just went on like that, without them knowing the first thing about me—like I didn't matter.

When I got almost to the highway, I could see somebody walking straight towards me from the other direction, walking real slow. When we got up close to one another and I seen his face, I liked to fell down. I said, "Isaiah?" but when I heard my own voice I felt like I had spoke out in a dream. "Isaiah Cutts."

The man kept walking.

"Isaiah, is that you?" I stepped up and grabbed his arm, but he jerked it loose and twisted sideways and looked me right in the face, straight at me, stared at me till I couldn't take it no more and I had to look off, and as soon as I did, he turned and went on down the road.

It was Isaiah Cutts, who I'd seen over and over again all those years, in my nightmares—Isaiah had come back. He'd been right there in the flesh.

And I felt something come out of me then, felt it fly out like a shock going the other way, and I started to run, and inside myself I was laughing and crying, but I didn't make a sound out loud, and I know somebody must have looked out their window and said, "There goes one crazy white man," since I took off like I was scared to death. I run as hard as I could, and I didn't even start to get tired, and I run through Cozy Town and out of it, and I felt like I could fly when I left the dirt road, when I turned and run straight toward the moon, where it sat down low over the highway.

7

After I'd served about half my time at the state prison, they put me out working on a road crew cutting weeds along the shoulder of the highway. They'd give us each a slingblade and they'd put a guard with a shotgun out there, and we'd work from right after sunup to nearly sundown. Most of the time I'd been locked up I'd had me a job working in the kitchen, and I'd pretty much got used to that, but then when some knives turned up missing, they cleared out everybody and put us on other jobs.

I didn't think it would make much difference to me one way or the other, but it did—going out every day and coming back in, I mean. Your whole world is made up of what's inside and what's

57

outside—that's the way you see everything; you got no choice. And as long as you stay in, you kind of get set. But then when you go out into the free world, it mixes things up. You're out, but not really, and then when they open the gates and the bus rolls you back in, it turns you inside out.

One day the bus took us a good ways down south of Milledgeville and put us cutting weeds on a stretch of highway that curved around Red Oak. To get there we had to pass through the middle of town, and it just eat me up inside. We passed right by the mill village, and I seen where our house used to be, where me and Susan and W.D. used to live. And we drove past the school where W.D. went too.

They put us to cutting weeds right down below where the dirt road that runs through Cozy Town comes out on the highway. Every car that come by us while we worked, I wanted to look at the people, and then at the same time I didn't want to look. I wanted to see a face I recognized from the mill, but then a part of me hoped I wouldn't. And as far as I know now, I never did.

There's something about the air of a place you start to recognize if you live there long enough. The way it smells and feels will be different from anywhere else. You might not be able to say exactly what it is—maybe the trees or weeds or the dirt or the breeze coming up from a creek—but it'll be all that or something like it, and a lot more, and you'll breathe it in and you'll believe there ain't no place else on earth that smells exactly that way, and it's right then that your heart might break, even if you're just a ordinary person walking down the road. But if you've thrown your life away for nothing—for an idea that, when you try to look at it, there ain't nothing there—and then if somebody's got a shotgun held on you, ready to haul you off and put you back behind bars, you can imagine what the smell of home will do to you—how it'll make you want to turn and run and keep going, so that maybe you'll take your last breath and you'll take it right there.

They held me for a year over at the state hospital, and then they put me in the regular prison. I didn't care where I was at.

At the hospital they'd give you medicine that made you feel bad, or they'd give you them shocks. They'd give you all kinds of tests, asking questions that didn't make no sense. Finally they got tired of fooling with me, and they shipped me out to the regular prison. Like I said, I worked in the kitchen and out on the road crew, except they'd always be having you do other things—something would need painting or cleaning. We dug ditches and unloaded trucks. They might have some construction they wanted you to work on, and I hauled a lot of block.

The harder the work, the better I liked it. The tireder I was, the less I had to think. I didn't want to think. I never took none of the books or magazines they'd bring around, since sometimes one of the pictures would remind me of Susan, and I couldn't stand to look at it.

I did read the Bible though. Not because I believed it exactly, but because I already knew what was in it, at least I thought I did. Preacher come around giving away these little Gideons that only held Psalms and the New Testament, and I took one, and I carried it with me till it fell apart and I got me another one. I'd carry it in my pocket, and when I'd be working somewhere and we'd get a break, I'd light up a cigarette and pull out my Gideon, and so folks got the idea I was big on religion. They didn't know I used it to keep from thinking. It did work for me at first, and even later on sometimes, but finally it didn't, except that by then I was in the habit of trying to use it that way and I couldn't quit.

I got me another book from the prison library that helped me pass the time too, and when I was in my cell I started to use that one. It was a book that give every word in the Bible in alphabetical order, and then it give the book and the chapter and verse where you could find it. It had everything in it, and I'm talking about every *a* and every *the* that's in there, it had them and where they were at. I got me a notebook and copied out lists of words and where you could find them, and then I'd turn to the Gideon and maybe I'd copy out the verse. I got me a full Bible to use when I was in the cell, so I could look up words from the Old Testament.

I'd just flip the book open and see what I come up with. I know there's folks think you can get a special message by doing that with the Bible, but I'm not one of them. Wasn't looking for no message in the first place. But it's true enough though, that when I flipped through the book, some of the words I seen there made me want to stop and look them up, while most of them didn't, and lots of times I couldn't have told you why there was a difference.

I looked up *window* and *promise* and *hill* and *salt*. I looked up names that I found there: *Ezra* and *Isaiah* and *Susanna*. I looked up *empty*. I looked up what the Bible had to say about animals—goats and swine and birds and cattle.

I seen how in the Psalms it says not to be like the mule, which has no understanding, it says.

I looked up *fire* and *yesterday* and *woman* and *rain*. I looked up *flower*.

I looked up *work*, and I seen in Isaiah where it says that the Lord will rise up angry to do "his work, his strange work."

8

I done told about Uncle Mack, my daddy's brother, and his sorry ways, but he was pretty much like his own daddy. Their mama, who I never knew—all my grandparents died before I was born— she went to a early grave from having too many children too fast. They say my granddaddy wouldn't hit a lick at a snake, but he'd beat my grandma regular, beat her with whatever he could reach out and get. My daddy talked about it once or twice. Said it was like his daddy would go crazy, and nobody could ever tell when it was going to happen. Said he remembered one night when his daddy was sitting at the table watching his mama cook supper, and out of the blue he jumped up and grabbed hold of a piece of firewood and swung it and caught her in the side and knocked her down, knocked the breath out of her. Never said nothing. Slung the firewood on the floor and then sat back down at the table and waited for his supper. My daddy said he could still see it: his mama laying on the floor with her mouth wide open, sucking for air, and his daddy sitting there like nothing had happened. Said that was the first time he remembered thinking somebody ought to kill his daddy. He kept looking at the pot of bubbling water on the stove and thinking his mama ought to grab it and pour it on his daddy, thinking maybe he ought to do it himself. But he didn't, and all she done was to get up and not say a word, knowing it could get worse. She just finished her cooking.

My daddy said he remembered how peaceful his mama's face looked when she died.

My daddy had one other brother besides Uncle Mack, but he died with diphtheria when he was a baby. They had two sisters.

When they grew up, one of them married a Bartow, and she lived out in Oklahoma, and the other one married a Waller and she lived down at the Florida line. Every now and then they would both of them come back and visit my daddy, but they quit doing that, and I never met none of them.

Mama's folks was sharecroppers in Alabama, other side of Eufaula. They had a first cousin by the name of Bolton Sims—they called him Cousin Bolt—and he owned land, and they sharecropped for him. They didn't have nothing of their own, Mama's folks didn't, so he let them live on the land, and because they was kin he treated them better than he would have somebody else. He let them work on thirds and fourths instead of on halves, which is the deal anybody else would have got.

Mama was the only girl in her family, and the youngest child. She had three brothers, one of which she never knew because he died before she was born, and as for the other two, there was times she wished they'd gone the way of their brother.

Mama was a sickly child, but that didn't matter to her big brothers, who enjoyed tricking her and teasing her and making her cry. One time they put a live roach in a biscuit, one of them big wood roaches with wings, and they each had them a biscuit filled with butter and molasses, and they started carrying on about how good it was, but said she couldn't have the extra one, which they had smeared some molasses on, and they pretended to try to keep it away from her, till she grabbed it and took a bite, and then the roach flew out.

And then there was Cousin Bolt. Every day the sun rose, he reminded Mama's folks of his Christian charity towards them. He didn't have no problem with walking in the house any time at all, day or night, since he reasoned he owned it. He'd walk in and start giving orders, talking about how they ought to scrub the floor more often, how the place had gone down since they moved in. Mama said her folks had to sit there and take it, since they didn't have nowhere else to go, but it was hard to swallow, since Cousin Bolt was one of these types that looked down on anybody that had to get their hands dirty when they worked, and he'd tell you as much, right to your face. Said God had made different kinds, some higher up than others. Said all you had to do to prove that was to look at the niggers, but that God had naturally put some white folks at the bottom too.

One late summer morning Mama's whole family had already ate breakfast, and her daddy and her brothers had gone off into the field, and Mama and her mama was about to go out there too, after they got the kitchen and house cleaned up. Mama said it was real odd, the way she felt at first. She started seeing things crooked. Like she'd look at a picture on the wall and go over to straighten it up, and then she'd turn around and see a pillow crooked on the bed, and then it looked like her mama's kitchen table had a slant to it, and then the door at the end of the hall started to lean. She went around trying to set things right, but when she seen the door start to fall sideways, it scared her, and that's when she felt it in her stomach, like somebody had hauled off and punched her with his fist as hard as he could. Her knees give way, and she went down, and she hollered out for her mama, who come running in and grabbed hold of her and dragged her up on the bed. But she couldn't lay down, she hurt so bad. She cramped up into a ball, and she felt her breakfast come back on her, and it spewed out of her mouth like a shot and splattered against the wall. Her mama had a wet cloth against her forehead, trying to hold her, but then all of a sudden she was crumpled up on the floor beside the bed, wretching and moaning too.

And they heard a noise like something hitting against the back door, and it turned out to be one of her brothers trying to get in the house, but he had fell out on the steps, too weak to manage it. They didn't know it, but her daddy and her other brother laid out in the field, flopping and gagging and shaking.

How long they stayed without help, Mama didn't know. She did know that a little while after she had fell out, Cousin Bolt showed up. He helped my grandma onto the bed and then he went out and drug mama's brother off the back steps and into the kitchen and left him laying there. Then he come back into the bedroom and said he was going into town to get the doctor, and he'd be back as soon as he could.

After my grandma threw up everything and went through the dry heaves and drunk water and lost that too but kept on drinking lots of water, she got where she could hobble around and see to the others. And then one of the neighbors stopped by, and when he found them all sick he drove his mule and wagon into town and brought back the doctor, who he found right there in his office, patching up a boy's cut leg—same place he'd been all morning.

The doctor said they was all poisoned, and he treated them as best he could. He found the bird dog dead out in the back yard and he asked what they'd fed the dog that morning, and they said they threw him out some biscuits.

He asked my grandma did she notice anything different about the flour she used that morning, and she said no, except that Cousin Bolt had come by and give them a sack of it last evening and had dumped it in the barrel himself.

The doctor done all he could and then left. Said he thought they'd all be fine after a while, except maybe for Mama, who worried him, the way her breathing stayed so ragged and the way her color hadn't come back. Bolt didn't show up again all day.

The doctor went back to town and talked with the sheriff, who played poker with Cousin Bolt regular and already owed him more money than he made in a year, and so when the sheriff done his investigation he decided it was my granddaddy that tried to poison his own family, even though he liked to have died from the biscuits too. They locked him up for two nights and while he was in there, Cousin Bolt come by and give him a talking-to. Said the best thing might be for them to pick up and leave, and when my granddaddy agreed to that, they let him go, and by noon the next day the family had loaded up everything onto the back of a wagon, had spent their last money buying a bucktooth mule from Cousin Bolt, and had started east for Georgia.

That left Bolt free to put some halfcroppers on his land and get a better return on it, which Mama said she guessed was all he'd wanted anyhow. She never did get over it, the fact that a man could find it in himself to try to kill off a whole family—kinfolks at that—like a nest of rats, but couldn't find the backbone to stand up straight and look folks in the eye and tell them what he wanted.

So they loaded up and got off the land. Mama still couldn't walk and still couldn't keep nothing down but a little chicken broth, and even that caused her stomach to cramp up real bad. But they loaded her onto the wagon along with what few belongings they had, and they headed down the road. Mama didn't remember too much about the trip, only that they'd stop and stay somewhere a while—folks might let them sleep in their barn and give them a bite of supper, and they might help out with somebody's crops for a day or two—but then they'd be going on, wanting to get as far away from Cousin Bolt as they could, and so they drove on a good ways into Georgia, and they settled down not too far from where my daddy and his folks lived.

And so my daddy was a Burt and my mama was a Sims, and somehow they met one another and fell in love, but they never did tell me that story. They had me, and they wanted to have more children too, but Mama couldn't, and so it was just us. And then just Mama and me, and then before too long, just me.

9

Isaiah was Otis and Essie Mae Cutts's oldest boy. They had three boys and four girls, and all of them had Bible names. You had Isaiah and Ezra and Ezekiel, and you had Mary and Martha and Sarah and Ruth. Ezra was about the same age as me, but we didn't play together too much. Him and Ezekiel, and the girls too, they always wanted to play ball and I didn't have no interest in that. They'd get them a old rubber ball and play with it till it split, and then they'd tape it up and play with it some more, till it fell apart. They didn't have no real bats. They'd use different kind of handles, broom or axe or pick handles, or they'd take them a length of board, like a two-by-two, and they'd carve them out a grip on one end, smooth it off real good, then swing that. I remember one time Ezra found him a real baseball in a ditch up at Ricksville, and he brung it home, and they tried to play with it, but it messed up the game, since you couldn't hit it good with the bats they had, and the ball was too heavy and too hard to be throwing all-out to somebody that didn't have a glove. And then too, they had a twist on the rules that let them get somebody out by hitting them with the ball. Instead of throwing the ball to somebody so he could tag the runner, they'd just aim for the runner. With a real baseball, if you played that way, somebody could have got hurt.

Neither me or Isaiah was big on baseball. I always had a hard time judging the ball since I was born with a bad right eye. It don't look no different from the other eye; I just can't see good out of it. That's the reason I never went to the war.

Isaiah didn't care nothing about playing neither, but for a different reason. He was the slowest moving human being I ever seen, before or since, so slow running the bases that even if he hit a long one over somebody's head, knocked it way out in the pasture—and Isaiah could do that, could knock the soda out of a biscuit—even then, they might get it back in and throw him out before he made it home. He was so slow it made folks laugh when they even thought about him running. One of the other children would start telling about Isaiah running, or else imitating him doing it—like Ezra used to do—and everybody would break up. Isaiah, he'd laugh too.

He walked slow and he talked slow, and if you asked him a question, at first you might have thought he didn't hear you, from the way he'd wait before he spoke. But he'd be thinking it over, and even if he was going to say, "I don't know," he might not say it right off, before he'd thought about it a bit.

He was about five years older then me, and I did have some questions about things, especially things I couldn't ask about at home without feeling funny. Me and him would go off down to the creek while the others played ball, and if they seen us heading out, they'd make jokes about how it would be dark before we got there, and such as that. Isaiah would just wave at them and keep walking. It was like he had some kind of heavy thing inside him that made him move so slow but also give him a kind of balance that other folks didn't have, and he didn't let the little things throw him off.

Isaiah was tall and lean, and real dark-skinned like his daddy. Their mama was a deep brown color, but their daddy was so black he had a kind of glow about him, and among the children, Isaiah resembled him the most.

And Isaiah was strong. The others might have teased him, but every one of them knew he could be trouble if you got him riled, which did happen, usually when he had to get in the middle of two of the others. They'd be going at each other, cussing and hitting and scratching, and Isaiah would step between them and take over. He had a way of taking you by the wrist so that if you moved wrong he'd twist it and you'd think it was going to snap, which it might have. He done it to me many a time, but only in fun.

And when it come to arm-wrestling, Isaiah could beat anybody. The way they told it, nobody had beat Isaiah since he was a little boy. They said he could beat his daddy from the time he was twelve years old, and Otis was way stronger than average. It got to where when Isaiah went to one of the stores around Yellow Shoals or up at Ricksville, somebody might just come up to him and ask was he the Cutts boy that could arm-wrestle, and when he said he was, they might want to take him on right there.

But if they did, it always come out the same way. Somebody that carried a lot more weight than Isaiah might look at him and believe that a boy as lean as he was couldn't beat them. So they'd set up and wrestle, and Isaiah would win.

One day a black man come through Yellow Shoals and wrestled Isaiah outside of Hodges Store, then went back to wherever he come from and talked about it, and the next week a truckload of black folks showed up over at the store, looking for Isaiah. I remember hearing about it from Uncle Mack, who was sitting there when they drove up.

"Niggers come riding in there, you could hear them coming a half a mile down the road," he said. "Wanted to know about that Cutts nigger that wrestles. The one driving said he'd wrestled him right outside the store there, so that's where he come back to. Hodges told them wasn't no Cutts nigger there. They asked did we know where he stayed. Hodges asked them was they fixing to buy something, and they quieted down, and then Hodges said, 'What y'all think my job is, sit here and keep track of niggers? If y'all ain't going to buy nothing, get your black asses on out of here.'"

Uncle Mack said the black folks rolled off real quiet, but when I seen them later on, over at the Cutts place, they was fit to be tied, cussing the white man who talked to them like that back at the store.

They had brought over a man nicknamed Big House, for reasons not hard at all to figure out. I don't reckon I'd ever thought folks could grow that big. He must have been close to six foot eight, and must have weighed every ounce of four hundred pounds, and didn't a bit of it look like fat.

I was over at the Cutts place because Mama had picked some good tomatoes and she wanted to give some of them to Essie Mae, and she'd sent me over there with them, and so I was walking into the yard when the truck pulled up, and that's when I heard them cussing and carrying on. But then they got respectful when Essie Mae stepped out and they seen her. They asked about Isaiah, and she told them yes, he stayed there, and she sent Sarah off to get him.

After a good while, here come Isaiah. One of the folks from off the truck said to Ezra, "That him?" and Ezra nodded. When they seen how slow he was moving, another one asked, "What the matter with him? He sick?"

Ezra said, "Naw, he ain't sick. Isaiah just don't get in no big hurry for nothing."

Somebody said, "House, look yonder. Look like he ain't got no meat on him at all. Don't you hurt the boy, now. Go breaking his arm."

Essie Mae was sitting on the front porch in her rocking chair. I walked over and sat on the edge of the porch. I looked back at her, and she winked at me, and then I remembered what I'd come over there for. I was still holding onto the bucket of tomatoes.

"Mama says these tomatoes is special."

Essie Mae took the bucket, set it down beside her chair, then picked up a tomato and felt of it. "You tell your mama she's mighty gracious."

"Yes ma'am," I said.

"Now, Chief," Essie Mae said, calling me by the nickname Isaiah had give me, and turning her attention back to the folks in the yard, "I don't reckon Isaiah ever wrestled nobody big as that one yonder. He some kind of giant, ain't he?"

"Yes ma'am," I said. "They call him Big House."

"Big House is right."

Turned out they didn't call him Big House because he was big as a house. They called him that because he'd been in the federal pen up in Atlanta, but we only found that out later on.

When he come in the yard, Isaiah seen it was the man he'd beat when they wrestled outside the store. They spoke, and then the man said, "Got somebody here don't believe you can whip him. This here Tyrus Bone. We call him Big House. House, this Isaiah Cutts. He say can't nobody whip him."

Big House put out his hand and Isaiah took it, but he shook his head. "Never said that." He spoke straight at Big House. "Never said can't nobody whip me."

Ezra jumped in and said, "Ain't nobody done it yet. Not nair one."

Big House looked around, and he said, "Where at?"

Isaiah pointed at the truck, walked over and put his hand down on the corner of the flatbed and said, "This look all right."

Big House nodded and started to take off his shirt, and when he got it off you could see he'd been in some other fights that wasn't supposed to be fun, like this one. He had the kind of skin that raises up when you cut it, had thick scars on his arms and his chest.

Isaiah stepped up to the corner of the truck and started to get his feet set, and then Big House stepped up, and they was about to lock hands when somebody yelled, "What the rules?" and the men backed off.

Somebody else said, "What rules? Ain't no rules. The one that put the other one down, he the winner."

Ezra spoke up. "They can't neither one raise up their elbow. They can't jump up on nothing. Can't lean way down and grab ahold of nothing with their left hand. Can't dig their fingernails in and try to cut the other one. They can do that, but they'll be fighting like a woman. There's your rules. Stick to them, can't nobody beat Isaiah."

They stepped up to the truck again, locked hands, and Ezra said, "Go."

Now this is what I remember. Big House's muscles popped and swelled out with the first pull. His arm made two of Isaiah's and then some. I had walked up closer to the truck, and I could see Ezra standing right there on the other side of it, and I swear Big

House's wrist was big around as Ezra's neck. You could see he was going to try to throw everything he had into his first move and beat Isaiah right off. But Isaiah was ready for him. He had told me about all the things folks try to run on you, thinking they can trick you. Said he wrestled all the time since folks kept after him to, but here somebody would come that didn't never wrestle, and they'd think they could throw something on him that he hadn't never seen.

I remember looking over at Ruth, the sweetest sister of all of them, but simpleminded. Isaiah always took special care of her, and she thought the sun rose and set on him, and when he started fighting the Big House, Ruth got all upset and started to cry. But then Essie Mae called her over and sat her up on her lap— even with her being as big a girl as she was—and talked to her, and Ruth got all right.

Big House put everything he had into that first move, and when Isaiah's arm stayed up straight, I seen the big man's face. He already looked mad when they started, but when Isaiah's arm didn't move, Big House shut his eyes and gritted his teeth, and when he done that, he looked like some kind of devil. Had two gold teeth, one on either side of his mouth—his dog teeth—and between them no teeth at all, just a space, and he had the tip of his tongue stuck through it.

He made another big push like the first one, and this time he let out a groan so deep you could feel it. And then I seen Isaiah's elbow slip to the side, just the least bit. I seen his arm angle back. Big House rose up on his tiptoes and leaned over, trying to get all his weight on top of his arm. Isaiah's back foot slipped, and his arm give a little more.

Everybody was yelling, and then I heard Otis say, "Hold him, boy. You just hold him, he'll give up." I didn't even know he was there, since he wasn't nowhere around when the wrestling started, but he'd come up behind us.

Isaiah's arm was bent back, but then when his daddy spoke up, you could see it start to move in the other direction. That ain't the pure truth. You couldn't really see it move, no more than you can see a shadow move when the sun goes to a different spot in the sky—it's too slow to see, but if you look and then you look back again, it's different.

I put it at about ten minutes after they started wrestling that they had their arms straight up again. Otis had gone over to sit with Essie Mae and Ruth on the porch. And then there come a stretch where everybody got quieter, and then things took off in another direction. The shouting picked up again, but this time Big House's own folks started cutting him. I heard one say, "What the matter, House? He too strong for you?" and then I heard some folks laugh.

One of them yelled at another one and said, "Reckon what we tell them when we get home? They ask, 'Who it was that beat the Big House?' and we say a skinny-ass nigger down at Yellow Shoals ain't got arms no bigger than your grandma's."

The whole crowd laughed, but I looked over at Otis and he wasn't laughing. He stood up and walked over and stood about ten feet behind Isaiah, and he said, "Boy, we got work to do."

He kept standing there, with his arms folded over his chest. I watched him a while, and then when I turned back to the wrestling I seen that Big House's arm had bent back about an inch.

I heard somebody say, "There he go, there he go," and then I seen Big House open his hand and pull his arm away, and he said, "I ain't studying this." He grabbed his shirt and walked around toward the front of the truck and crawled into the cab.

The crowd had been laughing and yelling, but all of a sudden they was muttering and cussing under their breath, and some of them looked a little scared. They got onto the truck real quiet, and we stood out in the yard and watched them go, and I remember how you could see the truck raising dust way on down the road.

Didn't nobody in Isaiah's family make a big deal about the match, at least not right then, but later on it turned out to be one of them things you measure time by—like saying whether something was before or after that summer Isaiah wrestled the Big House. And it got to be a story they liked to tell, and it was almost always Ezra that told it, and every time he told it, Big House got bigger and bigger. Ezra acted the whole thing out—played both parts and the crowd too—and when he got to carrying on that way, the whole family would fall out.

I've seen children like Ezra in other families, seen it in grown-ups too—folks that sort of take on the job of being a clown, like it's their job to lift everybody up when they need it, just by being a fool and forcing the others to laugh, even when they don't want to. And when I think back on it now, I can see it clear as anything, how when Ezra got going, that was the only time I ever seen his daddy let go, and I remember how strange his laugh sounded, and how it made it seem like it wasn't even him, like he was a whole other man, like he'd brought that laugh with him from somewhere.

It was about three summers before Isaiah wrestled Big House that he give me my nickname, while me and him was walking back from Yellow Shoals. Sometimes, instead of walking down the highway, we'd follow the creek. The water wasn't over knee-high, not even that deep in most places, so we'd roll up our britches and walk it.

That day we each had us a piece of rock candy, and hadn't either of us said much. We come around a bend and we seen a doe taking a drink out of the creek. Isaiah put his hand out and stopped me, and we stood there watching her. After a while she raised up her head and seen us, but she went back and drunk a little more and then she stood there looking at us with them big old eyes. We must have stayed there like that for at least a minute, not moving. And then a funny thing happened. When we first stopped, I'd said to myself, without really putting it into words, something like "Yonder's a doe," and when Isaiah put out his hand to stop me I said to myself something like "We going to watch her a little now," and after we'd been standing there a while, I said to myself, "All right, we done it. Now let's get on," but I didn't want to move until Isaiah said it was all right, and we waited and we waited, and then I said something to myself like "I could be one of them rocks yonder," and then I wasn't talking to myself no more. And what I realized when I thought about it later on was that right then I felt like I could have been the trees or the doe or the weeds on the bank or the light on the rocks the same as I could have been me. But all my talking to myself had stopped, and whatever I knew, I knew it the same way I knew the sunlight was flashing and breaking downstream because I could see it there, but I didn't have to say nothing about it.

When the deer run off, we walked on, and I had this feeling like I'd just woke up, and all sorts of things started coming into my head, and after a while I asked Isaiah did he know why a creek runs where it does instead of somewhere else; why does it end up going that one way?

Isaiah kept walking, studying the water, and then he told me how the creek runs out of the mountains, and then how it goes where it can, depending on how the land lays. Said he didn't know too much more about it.

"How long you reckon this creek been here?" I asked him.

He laughed at me then. "Boy, that like asking how old the dirt is."

I didn't want to admit right then that that was another one of the questions I was carrying around.

"Long time," he said, "but there ain't hardly no way to know, is there?"

"I reckon not," I said. "But don't you wish you'd been living a long time ago, back before there was stores or schools or roads— you know, back when it was the way God meant it to be?"

"Well now, I don't rightly know," Isaiah said. "You go talking about what God want, you got to be careful. Can't ever tell. He might like him a good road."

We come to some rocks and we decided to sit there and rest for a few minutes. Isaiah sat down and scooped up a handful of water and washed his face and rubbed it around the back of his neck, and then he cupped both his hands and leaned over and pulled him up a drink. The sun was coming slantways through the trees. I seen a snake doctor hover right where the water hit the rocks and kicked up a spray, and the sunlight cut across them both, so it put a shimmer on the snake doctor's wings, and where it caught the spray it made a little rainbow, and that was when I tried to tell Isaiah what I seen back there, looking at the doe. And while I was talking, Isaiah, he'd nod his head every now and then and he'd make a sound low in his throat like he was following what I was saying.

When I was done, there wasn't nothing but the ripple of the creek. And then in his own time Isaiah said, "You know what you sound like?"

"What's that?"

"You sound like a Indian."

76

"How you mean, a Indian?"

"The way you be talking about the creek and the woods," he said. "My mama got this cousin name Earl, up in Jackson County. When he come down, he always like to talk about how he got Indian blood, from his daddy side of the family. He kind of red, you know, and he say that the Indian part. Now Earl, we might laugh about him a little when he go home — Ezra like to say Earl, he don't know his ass from a hot rock — and there's lots of colored folk say they got Indian blood, you understand, but old Earl, he do know a few things. Got to give him that. And the way you be talking now, sound a little like Cousin Earl Indian talk."

I already liked the idea of being a Indian. I had me a box of arrowheads at home. I'd find them where we plowed, and some I'd found in the woods, and one of them I'd scooped up out of the creek right where we were sitting. And sometimes when I was little and I'd be playing by myself, I'd pretend to be a Indian. I fixed me up a bow and arrow, stripped a hickory limb, smoothed it and notched it and bent it, and I tied some string to it. And I made me some arrows to stick the arrowheads on, but I couldn't never get the thing to shoot straight. I'd crawl around real quiet-like, and then I'd jump up and shoot a arrow at something. For a while there, I shot the outhouse regular, till I done it while Daddy was in there and he learned me a lesson.

Isaiah said, "Sound like a Indian chief, what you sound like. Must be got you some Indian blood," and he laughed and reached over and pushed me on the chest so I almost lost my balance and fell off the rock backwards. Then he slapped me on the knee and stood up and said, "Chief, we got to get on."

We come out of the woods just above Mr. Stillwell's house, and we had to walk down the road a piece to get home. It was a big

77

white house, big as a church. I hadn't never been inside it then, and when we went by I said, "I sure would like to have me a house like that some day, wouldn't you?"

We walked on a ways, and then after a while Isaiah shook his head, but not like he was answering me. He was looking at the ground, and he just shook his head.

One time when Isaiah and me had took their wagon into town we stopped by the black schoolhouse on the way back, and we talked to Miss Roundtree for a minute. She was the only teacher I remember them ever having at the school, and she was one of the most proper folks I ever seen in my whole life. She was rail-thin and stood up straight as a flagpole, and she didn't talk like nobody I had ever heard, black or white. I wasn't even sure where she came from, but Isaiah told me later on she come from somewhere up North.

When we went in the school, which wasn't nothing but a old barn made into a schoolhouse, Isaiah took off his hat and made his greetings to Miss Roundtree, and then before he could say anything else she looked at me and asked him who his young friend was.

Isaiah said, "This here is Ellis Burt. His family work the farm next to ours."

She told him to say *this*, not *this here*.

Isaiah looked down at his hat. "Yes ma'am."

She said she was pleased to meet me, and she stuck out her hand. I took it, but I was scared to say much of anything, and I just said, "Yes'm," which I could tell by her eyes wasn't the right thing to say back, but she didn't tell me so.

Miss Roundtree asked Isaiah about his mama and daddy, and then she told him about how the other children was doing in school. I believe she mentioned Martha and Ezekiel.

We was about to leave when Isaiah asked her was there anything we could do for her, and she said there was, said she needed some wood split if we had the time. We walked out back of the school and got to splitting logs, and we worked at it about a half hour and was ready to quit when Miss Roundtree come up with a pail of water from the school's well. Isaiah was bent over and he didn't see her till she was right at him. She held out the dipper of water and he raised up and took it, thanked her, drank down most of it, slung the rest to the side, handed her back the dipper and thanked her again.

Then she stepped over to me, dipped some water out of the pail, held it out, and asked me did I care for some.

I was thirsty as all get-out, but I told her no thank you ma'am.

She give me a look—not mean or anything really, just a look—and then she slung the water out of the dipper, and she said she'd thought maybe I was thirsty too.

Isaiah seen what happened, but he didn't say nothing about it. When we finished, Miss Roundtree thanked us and then she give us each a piece of pecan pie she'd made. We both ate the pie before we got out of the schoolyard good, both of us glad to get it. I don't believe I ever had any better, but that piece sort of stuck in my throat, me being so dry, and I made Isaiah stop the wagon out front of Mr. Dempsey's place, and I run over to his well and got me a drink of water.

Down the road from us a piece there was two black families by the name of Tukes—Mozell Tukes and his family, and his brother James Tukes and his. Mozell had him a little farm that he owned outright, and he owned both the houses, his and James's.

Mozell had a dairy farm with two barns out back of his house. He'd painted his dairy barn white, and he'd repaint it just about every year. That barn was the first thing you'd see when you come up to the farm. Mozell said the whiter it was, the cooler it would be in the barn, and the cows would give more.

Mozell had four or five children, but I didn't really know them. His wife had died, and he was raising them by himself.

James lived about two hundred yards down the road from his brother, and he didn't have nothing of his own to speak of. Lived in a house Mozell owned, on Mozell's land. James had a wife named Pauline, and they had one boy, and his name was William.

James helped out his brother on the farm, but he mostly drank. You could go by there in the middle of the day and see him out on his porch with a jar of whiskey in his hand. And he was a bad drunk, a mean drunk, and he liked to talk, and he hated white folks. The few times I went over there with Isaiah, James lit into him for bringing me. He wouldn't say things directly to me, but to Isaiah, like I was such low-down trash he couldn't even stand to look at me. He'd ask Isaiah why he brought me over there. Said he didn't want no sorry-ass cracker on his place. One time when he seen me come into the yard, he stood up and threw a empty whiskey jar at me.

Isaiah said not to pay no attention to him, which is the way he handled it. We never went over there to stay long. We'd have some business, and when we took care of that, we'd head back. Usually we went down there to get butter, which Pauline made.

Mozell didn't have no use for white folks neither, but he didn't say too much about it. You could just tell by the way he'd look at you.

Ezra used to spend a good bit of time down there with James's boy William. They liked to go off into Yellow Shoals or Ricksville, if they could find them a way. William, he wanted to get off the farm as soon as he could. He had his mind set on living in Atlanta, and after that, he said he was going to New York or Chicago or somewhere up North. Said he was going to save up his money and then hit the road, and he wouldn't be back. Trouble was, he didn't make no money to save up. Mozell didn't pay him nothing for working on the dairy farm.

I reckon that's where it all started, with William. Him and Ezra went off to Yellow Shoals and got into trouble. They fell in with this black man that lived in Atlanta but was staying down in Yellow Shoals with his cousins for a while. He had him a car and he dressed up like it was Sunday every day, and then he didn't do nothing. Just sat around and spent his money, like he had a barrel of it somewhere.

Ezra and William was like a lot of young black folks who'd sit and listen to the man talk. Sometimes he'd give them a cigarette or a cigar. He'd tell them about Atlanta. Said you could go down on Auburn Avenue and go in as fine a place as any white man ever set foot in — restaurants, clubs, stores that sold fancy clothes just to colored folks. And the women, good Lord. Go in The Top Hat, he said, they'd be straight out of New York City, dressed all in silky tight dresses cut low so you could see what they had — women that knew how to treat a man, as long as you looked the part and could back it up and you had you some money.

Ezra and William got to where they couldn't stand it. They started to steal things. The man from Atlanta talked about how he knew folks that could take what you stole and sell it and not get caught. At first, they didn't really steal. They'd pick up stuff that they seen laying around, and they'd take it to him and ask could he get them folks in Atlanta to sell it for them. First thing they brought him was a man's left shoe and a old clay flowerpot, and they asked him could he sell them. Said the man laughed till he had a coughing fit and he give them both a dollar out of his own pocket and told them they was too country for this kind of work and they ought to go on back to the farm.

Two nights later they broke into a old woman's house in Yellow Shoals. She was off sick in the hospital and somehow they knew that, and so they busted out a window and crawled in. But the man from Atlanta was right. Ezra and William was not too smart when it come to sneaking around like thieves. They just went in and turned on the lights and started looking around, not thinking that if they knew the old woman was in the hospital, then her neighbor probably did too and might think there was something wrong about the lights being on. That's what happened, and the law showed up, but Ezra and William got away. They ended up with only a few pieces of fake jewelry.

After that, they'd try to steal something nearly every time they went into Yellow Shoals, and they got pretty good at it, and they started making some money. They started stealing things over in Ricksville too.

But word travels, and Otis and Essie Mae found out what Ezra and William was up to. Otis didn't whip Ezra right off. First he sat him down and told him a true story about a first cousin of his that white folks accused of stealing, but who hadn't done nothing except be a black boy. Told him how they put him on the chain gang when he was seventeen and how the boy never got off it; how he got so bitter he kept on getting into trouble with the guards and with other prisoners. Said he never come home, and they never did find out what happened to him.

Otis told Ezra this was what could happen to a black boy who hadn't done the first thing to deserve it. Told him to think about that, and then he took him out to the woods and whipped him with a stout hickory. Made Ezra strip down and whipped him all over—on his back and his legs and his shoulders. Said the boy couldn't hardly walk when he was through with him, and Otis carried him part way back to the house in his arms and turned him over to Essie Mae to doctor.

I know about this partly because Isaiah talked about it a little. But I know about it mostly because Otis talked to my daddy about it and Daddy told it to Mama and me. Said Otis started to shake when he talked about it; said he looked like he was about to cry but he never did. Daddy said he didn't know what to say to him, except that he done the right thing.

And Daddy told us something he hadn't told Otis. The story Otis had told Ezra about his cousin, and which he'd repeated to my daddy, that was a story my daddy already knew. He'd been in the courthouse the day they sentenced the boy, and then later on he'd heard from Uncle Mack what happened to him—something Otis didn't know about and which Daddy wouldn't describe to Mama and me. He said the boy was dead—that he'd died as awful a death as you could think of. Said it bothered him that Otis still didn't know exactly what had happened, but that he couldn't see no good to come out of telling him.

And my daddy was dead himself and buried in the red clay— buried in a corner of the graveyard at Missionary Baptist—that's where he was when I heard about what Ezra had gone and done anyway.

10

The cotton mill owned all the houses in the mill village, and they rented them out to the workers. The houses was small and the yards too, and some of the yards didn't have no grass on them. When we first moved in, ours had a few patches of scraggly grass, but that just made the yard look worse than if it was completely bare. Susan dug it all up and planted new grass and started her a flower bed.

At first she used seeds and bulbs she bought in town at the hardware store, and her garden looked pretty much like everybody else's, only bigger. And then as time went on she put to use what she'd learned from her Aunt Lenora about how to take wildflowers from just about anywhere and make them take root there in your own garden. Her aunt had made a real study of it and she'd passed it on to Susan.

We didn't hardly ever go for a walk or a ride without having to stop and look and maybe uproot or cut something or try to get some seeds.

It didn't take long for folks to take notice of how pretty Susan's flower bed was. She'd have flowers in there that nobody had ever seen anywhere except on the side of the road or out in a field or in the woods. And she'd put in what folks had only thought of as weeds, but when those flowered, they'd be as pretty as any-thing else.

I can't begin to tell you how she done it, only that it wasn't easy and it wasn't something that just come natural. One thing I do know is that her Aunt Lenora kept a notebook on her garden, and she had taught Susan how to do that. She'd write down everything about what she'd done—what the flower's name was; where she had got it from and when; what kind of dirt she'd found it in and if it was growing good there; how many she'd planted, and how many come up, and what they looked like and how long they bloomed and what kinds of seeds they dropped. She'd try out all different kinds of things, and she'd write down whether or not anything made a difference. People come around to see Susan's flower bed, and they went on about what a way she had with plants, like it was some God-given talent—which part of it surely was—but what they didn't know was how much of it was plain hard work that took paying close attention and writing things down and learning from what you done wrong or right the last time.

Anyway, Susan got a reputation as being good with flowers because her flower bed was always so pretty and because nobody else had one that looked anything at all like it. Mainly, she wanted it to look like it was all wild and had just sprouted up there, but without it looking too wild. She'd scatter the flowers and the weeds around and made the garden look like it had just happened. In her notebook, she'd write down how the flowers come up when they grew in the wild—whether or not they grew in clumps or was scattered around—and she'd try to make the garden look just the way it naturally would.

Every year the flower bed got prettier and prettier, and more wild-looking. Every year it had new colors and new blooms at different times of the year, which was one of the things she worked hardest at—to almost always have something blooming.

When the garden was about five years old, a man come around from the *Atlanta Constitution*. He'd been driving around through the countryside talking to folks and taking pictures for a story he was getting ready to do on people's flower gardens. He wasn't really looking in Red Oak but had just stopped off there to buy him a Co-Cola. Old John Carlyle down at the gas station had struck up a conversation with him and had naturally found out what he was doing there, what his business was, where he'd been, and where he was headed. If he'd stayed there long enough, old John would have got his shoe size and his middle name. When he found out the man was looking at gardens, John told him he'd better go on down to Fourth Street in the mill village and talk to Ellis Burt's wife and see what kind of flowers *she* had. So the man showed up and he took a lot of pictures of flowers and took Susan's picture and then in about two weeks there she was in the Sunday magazine, standing next to her flower bed. They just had a little bit on her—and two pictures.

The day that article come out, I've never seen nothing like it. You'd have thought somebody had died—cars all up and down the street, and a big crowd of folks out in the yard, most of them strangers that decided they'd just walk on up and take a look at the garden.

W.D. was about to bust, strutting around the yard with the magazine in his hand, going up to total strangers and saying "You want to see my mama's pitcher?" and then laying it out there for them, no matter how they answered.

I was real proud of Susan, but it didn't surprise me. I'd always known she was special. But all that attention made her uneasy. She went back in the bedroom. Folks kept asking if they could talk to her, and so I went back there and asked her, but she said no, and she told me to make all them people go home.

I went back out and I told everybody Susan didn't feel too good, and I said that if some of them wanted to come back another day, if they'd let us know before they showed up, maybe she'd be feeling better and could talk to them then.

Everybody cleared out, but that Tuesday Susan got a note from the Red Oak Garden Club, asking her to come talk to them about her garden. It was signed by Mrs. Rutherford, president of the club and one of the women Susan used to clean house for.

Susan said right off she wouldn't go, but she didn't write back. And then she got another note. This one asked could they come over to the house and look at the flower bed. Susan decided to go ahead and answer that one, and I thought for sure she'd told them not to come, till one Sunday morning she said they'd be there that afternoon. She'd told them she didn't want to have the whole club over to the house, but if a few of the women—three or four—wanted to come, that would be fine with her.

And so that Sunday we set up the card table and some chairs out in the front yard and she brung out a pitcher of lemonade and some paper cups, just the way she'd set up W.D.'s last birthday party. The women pulled up right on time, three of them, in a long black Cadillac that looked like the undertaker's, all of them dressed like they'd come straight from church. We had been to church that morning too, but we'd changed our clothes first thing when we come in the door.

Susan met them out at the street. Mrs. Rutherford give her a little hug and a kiss on the cheek, and she introduced her to the others—two other women, officers in the garden club. Susan led them over to the flower bed and showed them all what was in it, and then she brought them over to the card table and they sat down.

Mrs. Rutherford said she never would have thought she'd see Susan in the Sunday magazine.

Susan smiled at her, but she didn't answer.

One of the women—the youngest one, about Susan's age—said she was sitting there with the magazine and seen a picture of a garden in Red Oak, and she was wondering about it when she got a call from Mrs. Rutherford saying it belonged to a girl that used to work for her.

Susan was sitting up straight in the folding chair, feet together, and she held a cup of lemonade in her lap with both hands. She said, "I'm real glad y'all like my flowers. I really am."

The younger woman wanted to know where she come up with the idea for using wild plants in her garden, but then she went on to tell how she'd looked it up in some books and found out lots of folks had done it, and she wanted to know had Susan got it from a book.

Susan took a drink of lemonade and looked over at me, and I could tell she was ready right then for that afternoon to be over and done with.

Mrs. Rutherford said they was all wondering how she done it.

"It's just something my aunt taught me how to do," Susan told them. "She always raised flowers, and I learned it from her."

It was quiet for just a bit, and then Mrs. Rutherford come right out and said they wanted to pay Susan to come over to their gardens and teach them how to make a flower bed like hers.

Susan didn't think about it longer than it took her to swallow the drink of lemonade she had in her mouth. She said, "Mrs. Rutherford, I want you to know how much I appreciate y'all's offer, I really do. And I guess we could use the extra money, well I know we could, but I'm going to have to say no."

"Now, dear," Mrs. Rutherford said.

"No ma'am, you see, this ain't something I want to put up for sale. This is something my aunt showed me a long time ago, and it's special to me, and I don't believe I want to sell it."

The younger woman come back at her real quick-like, and with a sharp tone for somebody asking a favor. She said she thought

Susan was acting a little silly—said after all, it was just flowers—and she sort of rolled her eyes at Mrs. Rutherford.

Susan shot her a look but pulled it back. Then she stood up real slow and put her cup on the card table and smoothed her dress down and said, "I do want to thank y'all though. It's been real nice of you ladies to come by."

I seen how mad Susan was all of a sudden, but I could tell too that she didn't want to let the younger woman see it. She was just the type of person to go away and call Susan white trash because she'd got mad and started shouting.

"I hope y'all will come back again," Susan said real sweet, and she took a few steps in the direction of the street.

The women had to stand up and follow her then. When they got to the street and turned towards the car, the woman who hadn't said nothing reached back and touched Susan's arm and said something about one of the wildflowers Susan had got to grow. Said she didn't know how Susan had done it, but that she herself had never seen nothing like it, and that she was happy for Susan.

When we went back into the yard, I asked Susan which flower the woman was talking about, and she showed me, said it was a trillium, and she reached down and she cut two of the blossoms, and right then I seen she was smiling to herself. She gave W.D. and me one of the flowers each and made us sit down at the card table. The three of us finished off the lemonade, and then W.D. run across the street to play with Jerry, and Susan and me stayed sitting right there until the shadows started to come across the flower bed.

Right after W.D. was born, me and Susan started to go to church at Antioch Baptist, which most of the mill folks that was Baptist went to. It was only two streets over from where we lived. A wood building, about thirty years old, I'd say, and the only rooms it had was the sanctuary and two more rooms behind the pulpit and choir loft—a Sunday school room and a office for the preacher. I reckon there was about twelve rows of pews, so it wasn't a big church.

On Sunday mornings there would be preaching and the choir would sing a anthem, and they'd have all kinds of church business and announcements and so forth. Sometimes they'd talk about money, but they didn't use the word much. Talked about steward-ship instead, and tithes and love offerings and gifts. They always had a good crowd there on a Sunday morning, might even fill up the sanctuary.

But a Sunday evening was different. There wouldn't be that many people there. Sometimes the preacher didn't preach, or if he did, it would be more like he was just talking to you. Didn't hardly ever talk about money. On the nights he didn't preach, they'd have Bible reading and prayers, but mostly singing. On Sunday mornings they played a organ along with the hymns, but in the evenings they just used the piano, and I really liked that. You play a piano in a little church that don't have too many people in it, and where the piano sits on a wood floor and there ain't no rugs or nothing else to muffle the notes, and it'll give you a sharp, clean sound that I always thought was right for singing hymns with. Something about that sound cuts right through you, goes straight to your bones, and especially when it's a Sunday evening in the summer and they've thrown open the windows of the church, and you can breathe in what the cross-breeze might draw through—the smell of cut grass or the smell of a rain that's coming or one that's just passed, so it's wet down the dirt road. One of the sweetest smells there's ever been in this world is the smell of a dirt road after a rain.

I can't think about being at church on Sunday nights without Millie Reed coming to mind. I reckon she was about fifty years old when we started going to that church, but she'd been going there a long time. Even so, couldn't nobody say exactly what was wrong with her. She was touched in some way, that was clear enough, but didn't nobody know just how. She lived in a room over on Fifth Street, and she worked as a sweeper in the mill. She didn't have no family, and she never talked to nobody. You could speak to her and she'd look at you but wouldn't answer. Her eyes stayed kind of wide and scared-looking.

Millie never come to church on Sunday mornings, only in the evenings. She always sat by herself, in a spot that everybody knew to leave for her—fifth pew from the back along the right aisle. Like I said, she didn't speak to nobody. She just come in and sat there and didn't look around. If somebody come and sat on the same pew, she didn't look at them. She had this thing she'd do with her handkerchief. As soon as she sat down, she'd pull it out of her pocketbook—it looked like always the same handkerchief, a clean white one with a pink lace pattern on it—and she'd start to make this motion where she stuffed it all into her left hand and then she'd take the end of it and pull it out in quick short pulls until her left hand was empty. Then she'd stuff it into her right hand and pull it out with her left, and this went on the whole time she was there.

I used to watch Millie a lot during church, wondering what was wrong with her. I'd heard that one time, back when she was a young woman, she'd sat down at a checkerboard some men had set up on one of the loading docks down at the mill, and she beat everybody, coming and going. But she never said a word to them and she never played but that one time.

Sunday evenings there was always Millie and there was always singing. I've got what you'd call a ordinary voice, but I can carry a tune, and I used to love to sing. I never sang loud, not wanting to embarrass my family, but I sang every note of every hymn, and it always made me feel satisfied somehow, even when I was feeling bad.

And so on the evenings that we didn't have a sermon but mostly sang hymns, I felt glad to be there. I can tell you some of the ones I loved: "Whispering Hope," and "Wherever He Leads I'll Go," and "Softly and Tenderly."

The preacher chose the hymns, but the congregation did too, called them out, and you got to know folks' favorites. Like you could count on Sam Williams to want "Amazing Grace," and Ernestine Hobbs to ask for "Higher Ground." But there was nobody as steady as Millie Reed, and she never opened her mouth to make the request. Somehow it was understood, and it had been for many years, what she wanted. And so at some point in the service we'd sing "Sweet By and By." And everybody knew that we'd stand up to sing it. Some of the hymns we stood for and some we didn't, and there didn't seem to be a pattern to it. But we always stood for Millie's hymn, since she got to her feet right away, and so everybody else naturally rose.

Like I said, Millie never talked, never spoke a word straight out in the entire time I knew her. But when the piano started in on "Sweet By and By," she'd sing. And sometimes, because it was such a special thing to hear her voice, since this was the only time we ever heard it, folks sang real soft or not at all, and they listened to her instead.

When she sang, her hands got still. She quit pulling on that handkerchief, and she stood up straight and dignified, and when every other voice in the sanctuary fell away, it would be Millie alone—her and the old piano. Even the preacher stopped and listened to her.

And when she was done with that last verse, she sat back down real quick and started working her handkerchief, and for just a few seconds all we could hear was the noises of the night outside the church windows. But Millie's voice would still be going on inside us, singing the last notes of "Sweet By and By."

In that notebook Susan kept, she wrote down superstitions and beliefs and odd uses for flowers she'd heard about, almost all of them from her Aunt Lenora. She wrote down how the first lily was supposed to have sprung up where Eve's tears fell when she found out she was going to have a baby. She wrote that folks used to plant wild carrot on graves and that the Indians used bloodroot for warpaint. I already knew that last one. And I told her how my daddy would make up something for a sick mule out of bloodroot, but that too much of it was poison, and she wrote it down.

She wrote about how some flowers would keep their color and their shape long after they were dead, and so they got the name of Everlasting. She wrote how the mountain folk thought that if you pick the trillium it won't be long before it rains.

11

In prison I used to look up words that was only in the Bible one time. I was surprised to see that *belief* ain't in there but one time. You got *faith* all over the place, and *hope* too, but *belief* just that one time. Who would have thought that the word *piss* would be in the Bible more than the word *belief*?

Other words that's only in there once: *road* and *color* and *creek* and *mile*.

Cool ain't in there but twice, once in the Old Testament and once in the new. It's odd the way it shows up in the Old Testament, in a verse in Genesis where God's out walking through the garden in the cool of the day. Ever since I read that, I never could get it out of my mind—the idea that God would have been out taking him a walk late in the day when it's cool and maybe the sun is turning red out over the hills and gold where it comes slantways through the trees and catches the dust, and God stopping there to just look around him.

But then, the way the story goes, he had a reason to be where he was at. I thought about that a lot too. This was right after Adam and Eve had took a bite out of the apple—just two verses down from that—and so it looks like God come out there to talk to them about what they had gone and done. I couldn't help thinking it's mighty strange. There ain't but two people in the world, and right off, they get out of control.

I couldn't help but wonder about it—why God didn't make him a man and a woman that wouldn't go against him like these two. It almost seems like that's what he wanted, but then maybe there's some way he just couldn't do nothing about it.

Susan and me used to fight a good bit, but that was part of the spark between us—most of the time, that is. Sometimes I'd just start to pick on her, without really meaning to or wanting to or understanding why I was doing it, and then we'd have a different kind of fight. Like one night about a year before W.D. was born. I remember it was in the early summer, and how the smell of her

94

flower garden was coming in through the windows. We had just got up out of bed. Sometimes I'd see her come out of the bathroom after her bath, and she'd be wearing one of them silky nightgowns she had, and she'd pass in front of the window where the light slanted through, and I'd see the outline of her curves under the gown. She'd lay down with me and right at first want me to just hold her, and I'd smell her hair and her skin, which didn't need no flowery perfumes. Then she'd curve away from me and lay on her side and I'd turn and fit my body to hers, my lips touching the back of her neck where her hair fell sideways on the pillow, and I'd listen to her breathing and maybe I'd hear it grow regular and deeper and I'd know she'd drifted off to sleep, and I'd hold her there like that. And when her breathing changed and I knew she was awake again, maybe I'd kiss her real soft, and she'd turn and kiss me hard, and then all of a sudden none of this would be about satisfying me or her, but about satisfying some other thing we'd turn into when we laid down together. When that other thing started to move and make its own pleasure, I was awake everywhere on my skin and in my mind but gone deep in a dream too, and I was as careful and easy as I could be, but wild like a drunk man too, like I had clear whiskey warming me up and shooting through my muscles and bones.

And that evening we had just got up from being together that way, had turned one another loose and was separate people again, and we'd sat down at the supper table. We had some good tomatoes, and we'd fixed us up tomato sandwiches on white bread, with mayonnaise and salt and pepper; cut us up a cucumber and a onion and put the slices in a little bowl of watery vinegar and boiled us two ears of corn, and we'd each had us a glass of iced tea.

I remember how it come over me, near the end of the meal. We didn't ever talk a whole lot. Talked to each other more than to anybody else, but we still didn't say too much. And so we could sit there without talking and it wouldn't matter. Susan had her quiet spells and I had mine. But that night, close to when we got through eating, when she'd say something, I started to look at her different. I wouldn't even nod or raise my eyes or say "hmm" or "yeah" to let her know I was with her and paying attention to what she was saying. I reckon I got to sighing and just being quiet in a mean sort of way. I don't recollect exactly. What I do know is that it was enough to let her know something was wrong and to shut her up. And then I said, "There's this young girl starting on over in the cloth room, and I mean, she's something. You ought to see her. Men that ain't got no business in the cloth room starting to show up in there, just to get a look at her. It's right funny."

Susan kept on clearing off the table. I usually did my part of that, but this particular evening I stayed sitting down.

"Why do you think I ought to see her?" she asked.

She picked up my glass, which had about a swallow of tea left in it, and I reached over and grabbed it and said, "Hold on. I ain't finished with that," but I didn't answer her.

She didn't ask again, just went on with the dishes. I kicked back, put my feet up on the chair she'd been sitting on, and lit a cigarette. Susan was still smoking back then. She quit when she got pregnant with W.D. Usually when I lit a cigarette, I'd ask her if she wanted one, but that time I didn't.

"This old girl, I reckon she's used to it though. Women like that, they probably get used to it," I said.

She stopped rinsing the dishes then but didn't turn around, just stood there facing the window over the sink. "Women like what?" she said.

"You know, women that look like she does."

"No," Susan said, and she turned around and looked at me like I was a cockroach that had crawled out of the Quaker Oats box. "I ain't never seen the woman, Ellis. How exactly does she look?"

"Well," I said, "she looks a little like you, only she's built the kind of way that men are going to pay a bit more attention to her."

Men paid attention to Susan all the time. Sometimes I'd look at a dress she was about to wear to town and I'd want to tell her not to wear it, since it held her body real close. But then I'd realize it was just a ordinary dress and that whatever she put on, unless it was some baggy old thing, I'd have the same problem. And it was true. We'd be walking down the street and every man we passed would look at her, young and old. Some of them would look her up and down. I sort of liked it, but at the same time I couldn't stand it.

After I said what I did, she cut me dead. Didn't speak another word to me until I went to work, and that word was "Bye." I knew I'd hurt her, but I knew too, deep down somewhere, that that's what I was after, and I felt satisfied. I felt bad, but I was comfortable with it.

W.D. always got upset about us fighting. Sometimes when he'd hear us he'd start to cry. It scared him bad, from the time he was real little. We tried to tell him that sometimes two folks that love each other just fight a lot, the way me and Susan did, but that it don't mean nothing. We'd hug him, and we'd hug each other and try to show him everything was all right.

When W.D. got older—he started this around four or five—he took to hiding or running off when he heard us having trouble between us. He might hide in the tool shed out back or run across the street to Renfroe's house and ask could he play with their little boy. The first time that happened, it scared us to death. He heard us fighting close to midnight, yelling back and forth about money. When we quit, Susan went in to check on him, but he wasn't there. We searched the house, shouting for him, and we had both started to go wild when here come Renfroe's wife Alma in her nightgown, carrying W.D. across the street. He'd run over there and knocked on the door like it was three in the afternoon and asked could he play with Jerry.

I remember clear as day what I felt right before that, since for all I knew, W.D. was laying out in some field with his throat cut. I thought maybe I'd seen my boy alive for the last time, that he'd been taken from us without the least warning. You start to think like that, the worst sickness in the world starts to bubble up inside you. And even if you ain't a praying man or woman, let your child disappear in the middle of the night, it'll put the word Jesus in your throat, I guarantee it.

12

We ain't exactly what you'd call real close friends, me and Pete, but we do get along all right, which is a good thing, since it's a little house and I been living in it with him for about two years now. Pete, he likes to talk a right smart, but most of the time it don't bother me. It's more likely to be the other way around, meaning sometimes he'll get peeved at me for not answering what he's said, even if it don't need an answer.

He ain't the first Italian I've met—I've run into some every now and then since I got out of prison, in the different places I've worked—but he's the first one I ever spent any time with and really talked to. I call him Italian, but what I mean is that his mama and daddy come from Italy—and Pete's got lots of stories about that, about when they got off the boat and how folks treated them and what a hard life they had—but Pete himself was born over here. Him being Italian and me spending all my life in Georgia, there's lots of things we don't look at the same.

Take food. We can both cook pretty good, and so we'll trade off on the cooking, but it don't always work out. I run across some fresh collard greens one day—bought them off a truck parked down by the mill—and the next morning I started boiling them down. I've always thought that to get them right you got to cook them most all morning and then some. They do have a smell to them, but I grew up with it and it don't bother me in the least. In fact I like it, but it run Pete out of the house, and he didn't come back until about suppertime. I'd told him I knew it smelled strong, but it was one of the best things he'd ever eat. I fried up some fatback to eat with the greens, and I made us some cornbread for sopping up the pot liquor, and I'd cooked down some tomatoes with sugar, and I set us out some clear pepper sauce and some iced tea, but after all that Pete still didn't care for none of it. He tried it, being polite, but he made himself a sandwich later on.

But then too, I can't even really tell you what he laid out on the table one night—another one of them things with noodles he likes so much, only this time the noodles was green and they tasted kind of spoiled to me, and the sauce you poured over them was white instead of red, and it tasted fishy, and I just couldn't make myself eat it. But Pete, he thought it was the best thing in the world, the same way I did with the collards.

And there's other things, like the television. Pete's got him a little television that looks like it was the first one they ever made, black and white, and he likes to sit right up close and talk back to it. He likes to watch the news two or three times a night, and then he likes to watch all these shows that ain't nothing but other folks talking about the news. Sometimes he'll whirl on me and want to know what I think, and half the time I ain't been paying attention.

He don't do it so much any more, but Pete used to really get riled, talking about what a sorry state the country's in. He said you got folks that don't want to do nothing but sit on their rear ends and draw a check, while other folks are out there working and paying taxes. He draws a check too, but he said he'd give it back if he could afford to. Said he didn't feel right taking a dime he didn't work for.

But some folks nowadays, he said, they act like you owe it to them. Like if they put out their hand you're supposed to lay some money in it, and if you don't, they'll get all righteous about it.

He said you got folks sneaking into the country so they can get help from the government, and the government goes ahead and gives it to them—free doctors and food and schools, on and on.

He don't talk that way as much as he used to, but he still goes on about other things and how they are now, how they ain't like they used to be—back when you could leave your house unlocked and wouldn't nobody bother it, back when children was respectful, back when the schools taught them something, way back when a dollar was a dollar.

He goes on talking about the old days, and he's partly right I know, but to me it's a hard thing to do—to dwell so much on what's gone and won't ever be the same again, even though I ain't thinking about the same things he is.

One thing Pete likes to do is drive. He'll get in that old car of his and drive all over the county, not looking to get nowhere especially, but just to see what he can see. He likes to drive mostly early in the morning or late in the afternoon, but he always wants to get back home before the news comes on, since that's such a big part of his day.

Sometimes when I wake up in the morning he'll be gone already—either to the morning service over at the Catholic church or just out for a drive—but he'll always be back in time to carry me to work. Every now and then he wants me to go with him, and so I do. He likes to roll down the windows and drive real slow and try to look at everything, which makes him dangerous on the highway. He drives like he thinks they painted them yellow lines on the road for decoration, and I've told him so.

Pete's a real talker, but when he gets in that car and starts to drive, he don't talk much at all, unless something happens to set him off, and he never does turn on the radio. I thought it was broke till I tried it one day when he went in a store to pay for gas and it come on.

Pete likes to go down roads he ain't ever been on before, and we've ended up at dead ends and washouts and in folks' driveways. Don't neither one of us like to ask for directions, so we drive on till we find out where we're at.

I'd been living in his house about a year, I guess it was, when we drove down Rutledge way, turned off and went up a road toward Hard Labor Creek, where the sign said there was a park. We didn't care nothing about going to a park, but we drove on to see what it was. We rolled on in there and didn't see nobody at all. There was some shelters with tables set up on concrete slabs, but nobody using them. We drove down to a parking area and pulled in there and got out, but wasn't a single other car there. From where we stopped, we could see the beach, only about fifty yards wide, if that, and wasn't nobody on it, and nobody was swimming either, which didn't surprise me at all, since the water was as red as the dirt path leading towards the beach.

We got out of the car and walked down the path. There was a old bathhouse off to the left—one part of the roof caved in, glass broke out of the windows. From there we could see a lot more of the lake, and it was one big mudhole, and nobody on it, not one boat. Just the other side of the bathhouse was a little playground with two big swing sets and a seesaw, but the swings didn't have no seats in them and the chains hung free, and the seesaw was twisted sideways.

"I guess we got here a little bit late," Pete said. He pointed toward a dock half falling into the lake. "A few years, I'd say."

Later on we found out there was a new park down the road a ways, and that nobody ever used this one now. But you could tell it had had its day. All around the swing set and the seesaw there was deep troughs cut into the dirt by children's feet. And you could see initials and names and hearts cut into the walls of the bathhouse, and signs for refreshments still hanging there. Out in that muddy water there was a platform with a slide and a diving board, and on the beach a lifeguard chair laying on its side.

I seen something move off to my right, and when I looked, it was a young man and woman laying half-hidden on a blanket just where the beach left off and the grassy slope started. They'd been having a picnic there. I seen a cooler and they had food laid out all around them, and I could make out what looked like a wine bottle. The woman waved at us, and we waved back, but then we turned and headed for the car.

We drove on out of the park and went off in the opposite direction from the way we'd come. We must have gone about five miles when we hit a long line of cars where the state patrol had set up a roadblock to check licenses. We sat there for maybe two minutes, and then Pete said, "I don't believe I'm going to waste my time like this," and he started backing up, till the car behind us blew its horn. Pete waved at the driver, then swung a hard left till he was completely crossways in the road, which was only a narrow two-lane with a shoulder that dropped off sharp on either side. He worked the car back and forth till he got it turned and headed back in the direction of the park, and he drove on off.

We were headed due west then, the clouds in front of us lit up different shades of red and gray, layers of clouds, so that some looked close and some far off, and if you let yourself see it, it looked like the land going on, up there in the clouds.

"Well," I said.

"Well what?"

I hadn't really meant to say nothing out loud. "I was just talking to myself," I said.

He wanted to know what it was that I'd been fixing to say to myself, and he was looking at me now like I was a child he'd caught in a lie, just a trace of a smile coming to him.

"Well," I said, "I was wondering if you can do that, that's all."

"You just saw me do it, didn't you?"

"It ain't against the law? That's what I always heard."

Pete didn't have to answer me, because all of a sudden there was a blue light flashing behind us and a state patrolman pulled us over and got out and wrote Pete a ticket, all sort of matter of fact. Told us to have a good day and went on back towards his roadblock.

It surprised me that Pete didn't argue with him, just took the ticket and put it in his pocket and drove on off, all real calm.

About two miles down the road Pete said, "Let's see what she can do," and he put his foot to the floor, and the old car roared and jumped and threw us back in the seat, and we come to a curve and Pete almost lost it, the right back wheel hitting the dirt, but Pete keeping his foot to the floor and everything going by in a blur, and then just like that, quick as he started it, he slowed down. And he was laughing.

But it wasn't funny to me. I said, "Just let me tell you one thing right now, and I'm real serious about this, and I wish you'd listen to me: that right there is not the way I want to die."

Pete laughed harder, and he threw his head back, like he'd forgot he couldn't do that, and it hurt him and he grabbed his neck and nearly went off the road then too. He drove on and hit a highway he recognized and before long we reached home, just in time for the TV news.

13

William and Ezra got them a partner out of Ricksville. He come down to Yellow Shoals and picked them up in his wagon and carried them to Ricksville or somewhere else so they could break into houses or stores, and then they split the money they got out of it.

They'd come into Ricksville and leave the mule and wagon in the woods south of town, where the swamp started and there wasn't many folks around, and they'd walk on into town. They'd walk in one at a time, putting about five minutes between them, so as not to draw attention. They got to be pretty good at figuring out whether somebody was home or not. They tried to stay away from any place that had a dog. They sat out in the woods behind houses and watched what went on, and they learned that some folks will make it easy for you by going off somewhere and leaving a door standing wide open. Ezra and William had got smart since they fell in with this other boy, and he was a boy too, just like them—no older than sixteen. They didn't take no chances now, at least if they could help it.

After they'd hit Ricksville a good many times, they figured it was too risky to keep on, and they started looking for another place to work. The problem was, they didn't have nowhere else to go. If they'd had them a car, it would have been different. They could have gone over to Simpson or Crow Valley, but it was too long a ride for a mule and wagon.

So that was when they hatched their big plan: they'd find a way to rob Mr. Stillwell. If they could get into his place, there was no telling what they'd come away with. They figured they'd be able to go on to Atlanta right away, and maybe even on up North. And it made a lot of sense too, Mr. Stillwell being the richest man in the county, and them living right there close to him, so they could watch his house and try to see was there a regular time when folks would be there and when they wouldn't. They watched to see if somebody stayed there when they went to prayer meeting on Wednesday night or to church on Sunday morning. They noticed that Mrs. Stillwell had a club meeting she went to every Friday night—some missionary society—and that sometimes she'd take the baby along with her, and then if Mr. Stillwell went off down to Hodges Store, like he did almost every night, there wouldn't be nobody but Alice and her sister in the house, and they went places too.

One of the boys would go down to Hodges Store and sit outside beside the screen door drinking a Co-Cola and listening to Mr. Stillwell talk, in case he said something they could use, which he finally did. He got to talking about his worthless brother-in-law over in Crow Valley, and he said his wife always seen the man as her little brother, even though he was forty years old, and every now and then she'd have to go over there and wipe his nose for him. Said she was going over there that Saturday and was taking the girls with her.

William heard him say it, and when he told the others, they knew it was their big chance. The other boy said he was going to find him something to drive so they could get away fast. They got everything they wanted to take with them to Atlanta all packed up and ready to go, and on Saturday night they met up over at William's house, and after it got dark they drove the truck that the other boy had got his hands on to a spot about a half mile from Mr. Stillwell's house and they pulled it down into a logging road and walked through the woods.

Mr. Stillwell had two cars, and neither one was there. A light was burning on the porch and another one in the middle hallway, but besides that, the house was dark. The three boys sat in the woods and watched the house, leaned back against pine trees, and waited. They didn't say nothing, just sat there holding onto the croker sacks they had brung along to carry things off in.

After they'd sat there about a half hour and didn't see nothing, they figured it was safe. They walked around the house, and they seen two windows open a little at the bottom, and they crawled in the one at the back. They had talked it all out before, and their plan was to try to find the jewelry box in Mr. and Mrs. Stillwell's bedroom. They had a good flashlight they had stole out of a house in Ricksville, and they stayed real close together while they went through the house. They'd learned not to get cocky and take things for granted, and so they didn't make no moves they didn't have to, and when they opened the door to a room, they stood there and shined the flashlight all over the room to see if there was any reason to go on in.

They figured the main bedroom was upstairs, so they went on up the steps. The first room they come to was the Confederate museum. It had a saber hanging on the wall, and uniforms and hats and a old pistol, and a big picture in a frame almost as tall as a real man. Something about it struck Ezra as funny, even though he knew it wasn't the time to be laughing, but he couldn't help it, and he laughed so hard he had to put his hand over his mouth. The others stood right where they was at until Ezra got hold of himself, and then they went on into the next room, which wasn't the Stillwells' room either, but Alice's room, where she was in her bed asleep till they opened the door and shined the flashlight on her, and she screamed.

Ezra and William turned and run down the stairs and out of the house. They couldn't see where they was going, and they knocked over tables and vases, knocked mirrors and pictures off the walls, and Ezra run into something that caught him on the side of his face and cut him real deep.

Ezra and William had hit the woods before they knew the other boy wasn't with them. They turned around and they seen a light on in a bedroom next to the one where Alice was. They didn't see no light in her room. They stood there holding onto their empty croker sacks, staring up at the house, and then they turned and run through the woods, as hard as they could, and when they come to the truck they grabbed their things out and kept on running.

Ezra stopped off at the creek and tried to doctor his face a little. Wet down one of his shirts and cleaned out the cut and tried to make it quit bleeding by pressing the wet shirt tight against it, but it was a mean cut and it went deep, and he couldn't get it to stop.

When he got home, he sneaked into the house and woke up Isaiah, who took him out to the barn and held a cold clean rag against the cut and then got him a long curved needle and some fishing line and sewed up the cut the best he could, with Ezra cussing and crying and pulling away and fighting him. After he was done, Isaiah poured some of that purple medicine they used on the cows over the stitches, and Ezra like to have passed out.

And then Isaiah made him tell everything that had happened, and when he told how they'd left the other boy in the house, Isaiah jerked him up and they took off, and it was hard for him to keep up with Isaiah while they was running, old slow Isaiah, and when they got to where the truck had been, it was gone.

And so they turned around and went on back home. Where Isaiah had sewed up Ezra's face, it kept on bleeding, and Isaiah said he thought they'd best tell their folks and see could Essie Mae do something. Said he didn't know what he'd been thinking anyhow, he should have took Ezra straight to them in the first place.

"Here I go acting crazy as you," Isaiah said. "Got a cut down to the bone and you and me sneaking around like we was going to hide it."

Ezra begged him not to wake them up, said when his daddy found out, no telling what he'd do to him.

Isaiah said, "You best get your mind on Mr. Stillwell, boy. He catch up to you, you'll be hollering for your daddy."

Ezra said there was no way that would happen, since they'd planned everything out real good and didn't leave no evidence. He said him and William run out so quick the girl never got a good look at them, and the other boy, he'd be long gone now and he wasn't the kind to open his mouth. And anyhow, they hadn't really done nothing, hadn't even took nothing, just broke in the house and got scared off when they woke up Alice and she screamed. Said he figured they was in the clear now, and so he didn't see no reason to tell Otis and Essie Mae the whole truth.

"We just tell them somebody over in Yellow Shoals cut me in a fight. Just tell them that."

But Isaiah said, "You better wake yourself up, nigger. Time the sun come up, the law going to be out, looking for the boys that broke into Mr. Stillwell's house and busted in on his girl."

Isaiah told Ezra he'd probably bled all over everything trying to get out of the house and they'd be looking for somebody with a fresh cut, and he sure enough had one. Said he'd better hope they could find a good place for him to hide.

So they went in the house and woke up Otis and Essie Mae, and Isaiah told them what had happened and he put a lamp up to Ezra's face for his mama to study it. She said the stitches looked passable, but that he might ought to have put some more down in the muscle and then another one in the skin, since the cut had gone so deep. But it was too late now, she said, unless it kept bleeding bad and they had to tear out the stitches and do it again. So she washed it off and doctored it some more.

The whole time since they had come in, Otis hadn't said a word. After he'd got a good look at where the boy was hurt, he'd gone across the room and sat in a straight chair and listened to the story Isaiah told. Sat with his bare feet flat on the floor and his hands folded in his lap. And then, after Essie Mae had cleaned out the cut and put some of her medicine on it, Otis got up and walked outside and stood in the yard.

Isaiah sat by his mama while she held the cloth on the cut, and she asked Ezra questions like what happened after they run out of the house. Did the other boy steal anything and did he do anything to Alice was what she wanted to know, but he said he didn't know.

Otis hitched up the mule, and they put Ezra in the wagon and Isaiah and Otis drove him over to Simpson, where they had people, and then they turned around and come straight back, and the sky was red between the pines by the time they reached the farm. They went straight to milking, and after that Isaiah went back to the house and got his breakfast from his mama like always, but Otis stayed out, and Essie Mae took a ham and biscuit out to where he was, but Otis wouldn't touch it, and she stood there with him while he leaned on a fence post, stood behind him with her arms wrapped around him and her head laid against his back, and she could feel his breathing, and for a long time, they just stood there.

Alice said there was three colored boys, but it was too dark to say if she knew any of them. Two of them had run out of the house right away, but the other one put a pillow over her face and tied her hands behind her and then made her lay face down while he blindfolded her with one of the pillowcases. She said he'd gone off into other rooms looking for things. She could hear him opening drawers and turning things over. She said it all happened real fast, and then she heard the boy running out of the house.

When Alice come to school Monday morning, folks walked around her like she had the smallpox. They looked at her real close to see if they could tell. The children whispered back and forth what they heard their folks whisper at home, wondering whether or not Mr. Stillwell would take her up to Atlanta, where they did them sort of operations. Some of the girls said they'd just go on and die if it happened to them like that, but then they wondered if after he started doing it to her, Alice got to liking it.

Mr. Stillwell was already set to kill somebody, but he hadn't done nothing except have the sheriff start investigating all over the county. And then Alice went to school, expecting folks to understand that she'd got scared real bad, but she was all right now, and ready to forget about it as much as she could, even though it did make her cry sometimes when she thought about it.

The first day when she come back, she seen how folks stood off from her and how they looked at her—me too, she said—and she wanted to know why. I told her I didn't know. Said I reckoned folks felt bad for her and didn't know what to say. What about me, she wanted to know, since I'd told her right off I felt bad about what happened to her?

I couldn't give her a good answer. "I ain't acting no different," I said, but I heard myself say it too loud and almost like I was mad at her, and she heard it too.

I didn't believe that what folks was saying was true, but just the idea of it made my skin crawl—her and some black boy. That's how I felt, and I couldn't help it—that's how I was raised. Even if I'd been thinking of her and Isaiah, that's how I'd have felt.

Didn't nobody think blacks and whites ought to be getting with one another, at least nobody I knew, white or black. Even my teacher, Mrs. Partain—who was so big on teaching us to have manners—she'd get off talking about how it was one thing being equal under the law, which she believed blacks and whites ought to be, but it was another thing being equal in society, which she thought was wrong. She said you had to respect everybody, but that there was good reasons against mixing in society.

I happened to be watching when Alice found out what people was saying. One of the girls went up to her and whispered something, and all of a sudden Alice started running, and she run on out of the schoolyard and down the road.

And when she got home and told Mr. Stillwell what folks believed, it might as well have really happened just that way.

14

While W.D. was a baby, Susan stayed home with him, but after he was older she got restless. Even before then, she never was one to sit still—always scrubbing and washing and cleaning and mending. In a four-day span she scraped and painted the house. She had her flower bed, and back behind the house she put us in a little garden with a few rows of corn. She put in some squash and tomatoes and okra, and she raised them hot little finger peppers.

Now she done all this while W.D. was still real little, but later on, even all this work couldn't hold her. I reckon she had her Aunt Lenora to go by, and for her Aunt Lenora, according to what Susan had told me, every day was something new. That woman would go out through the county and into some of the neighboring ones looking for cast-off valuables, and there was no telling what she'd find, and not just in the way of things to buy and sell. Say you come up on this house, she told Susan, and there's three miserable burnt-out pots, a yellow lampshade, and a pair of brogans sitting out in the yard beside a big cardboard sign that says "For Sale Bargain." There's bound to be a story with some trouble behind all of it, she told her. And if she stopped the truck and asked about the things for sale and then sat and talked a while, she'd hear it. Susan said her Aunt Lenora taught her that all you need is for somebody to lay their hand on something and start talking, and that thing will change.

Now you might think that having been raised this way, Susan would have been big on saving things, like keepsakes of when W.D. was a baby—things like baby shoes and locks of hair and so forth, and maybe especially pictures—but she didn't care nothing about them things. It was me that put some of them away and me that would haul out the Kodak to take their picture, and me that carried a snapshot of the three of us in my billfold.

Susan was partial to what was alive, what she could see growing, like a ear of corn, or a tomato vine, or a showy primrose she'd brought in off the side of the road and made to grow there in her flower bed.

I made pretty good down at the mill, what with all the overtime I was getting, so there wasn't no need for Susan to work, but like I said, she got restless. She stayed home with W.D. till the year before he started school, and then she made a deal with Alma to keep him for a part of every day. Their boy Jerry was the same age as W.D., and W.D. played over there so much of the time anyway, it seemed like a natural thing to do. She paid Alma a little, and Alma was glad to get it.

Susan got her job as a waitress over at Stanley's Café. She could work short hours there if she wanted to, could work morning, afternoon, or evening if she set it up. She liked the woman that owned the place—Rose Collins, who reminded me of Mrs. Kilgore, only a lot older—and she pretty much liked the other waitresses, and the work kept her busy, and she liked having her own spending money.

But I don't believe it was the money that made her want to do it, and it wasn't because staying at home and doing her work there and taking care of W.D. wasn't enough to wear her slap out. I think she had this yearning to keep on doing things that was different—not exciting or better, but just different—and it worried me sometimes, made me wonder when she was going to want somebody different from me.

Miss Rose, which is what everybody called her—she was about eighty and had run the café for close to thirty years since her husband Stanley died—she used to come over and sit with me when I'd come in there for a cup of coffee. We had a running joke, since she'd flirt with me and give me all kinds of sweet talk so Susan could hear it. She always went on about how me and her was planning to run off together. The truth is, you could look at Miss Rose and see she still had some fire in her. And once or twice when she slid into the booth and started her teasing, run her hand up behind my neck, I could tell just by what I felt in her hand and by the way she moved when she done that, that this wasn't no dried-up old lady, but a woman that understood exactly what she was doing. All the waitresses there sort of took after Miss Rose, and they'd flirt with the men like that was part of the job, and Susan acted just like the rest of them.

Miss Rose let Susan change her hours around, depending on what shift I was working at the time. She mostly worked in the mornings and afternoons though, since didn't neither one of us want W.D. to be staying with somebody else at night, the way it would have been if I was on second shift or had got overtime. She liked working at the café in the mornings when the breakfast crowd come in. The work was faster, the tips better, and she said something about a morning crowd kept up her spirit. She liked working afternoons pretty well too. W.D. always took him a good nap in the afternoon, and so for part of the time he wouldn't even know she was gone. And sometimes she liked to have her mornings free to work in the yard and in her flower bed. In the summer, if you didn't get out there early, before noontime, the heat would knock you out.

I come in one afternoon and I seen Susan sitting in a booth across from this man. He was a big man, and not a bad-looking sort, eating and talking at the same time. I walked up to the booth and said, "Hey."

She hadn't seen me till I spoke. She said, "Oh hey, baby," and she pulled me down onto the seat beside her and grabbed my hand under the table.

"Charlie, this is my husband, Ellis," she said. "Ellis, this is Charlie Ross. Charlie always comes in when he's passing through. He drives a truck, and he was fixing to tell me about something. Go on, Charlie."

The big man was bent over his plate, sopping up some gravy with a roll. He nodded and wiped his hand off on his napkin and reached over, and we shook, and then he started back talking.

He said he was out near New Orleans, on the other side of it, had a load of scrap he was carrying out to Galveston, and he come up on a wreck, where a pickup truck had rammed the side of a car carrying a woman and a little girl about four years old. The car had flipped over, and the woman was laying in the front seat dead, and the little girl was screaming and crying. He was the first one on the scene except for the driver of the pickup, who had a broke leg and had crawled out of his cab and was laying there on the side of the road. The car had landed on its side and was wedged down in a ditch. He said he couldn't see how you could turn it back over, and the door you could get to was where the truck had hit it, and it was all smashed in.

The man said he'd seen some bad things, back in the war, but that really got to him — that little girl screaming and all.

Susan was gripping my hand under the table.

The man said he seen what he had to do. There was no way to get that little girl out but to break a window and reach in over the woman and get her. The back seat was jammed full of things, so she couldn't come out that way, and the seats had been slung all around, and the woman was wedged up and back against the window, and she was partly blocking it.

He went back to the truck to get a crowbar to break the window. By that time a lot of people had stopped and the traffic was starting to pile up. There was a crowd around the car. He started to swing away at the window — hit it twice, and the second time he swung the crowbar it hit the woman in the back, and she moved a little and called out in a weak voice. He said he would have bet a thousand dollars the woman was dead, from the way she was laying, and the way her neck was turned, and from how much blood she'd lost, and how still she'd been.

He said they almost had her shoulders through the window when the car caught on fire, and the smoke got bad, and then all of a sudden there was fire everywhere, and they had to let the woman go.

The man looked down. "She didn't scream too long," he said, but he said it was the worst thing he'd ever heard in his life. Said there was this beating and thumping around from inside the car.

His voice broke off, and Susan let go of my hand and reached over and laid her hand on top of his. She said, "You done all you could, Charlie," and what I heard in her voice then made me feel queasy in my stomach—because what I heard was a voice that I knew it took a while for Susan to get around to, a voice I'd never heard her use with nobody but me and W.D.

I took another close look at the man. You could see his muscles through his shirt. He had hair that was wavy and slicked back, with streaks of early gray along the sides. And from the way he talked, I knew he'd been to school.

Maybe I was acting childish—I know I was, after the story he told—but I couldn't sit there and listen to Susan use that voice with another man, no matter what he'd been through. I stood up—not real fast, but I got up—and I said, "There's somewhere I need to be."

Susan pulled her hand back, and then she looked at me, I swear, like I was a stranger. "Where's that, Ellis?" She didn't hardly ever call me Ellis unless she was mad at me.

"Some work I ain't finished," I said. "I'll be home after a while."

"Some work?" she said.

"That's right."

As soon as I stood up, I wanted to sit back down, since I knew I was acting like a straight fool, but I walked out and went on down to Ramsey's Pool Room, the whole way telling myself I was a grown man, why couldn't I act like one, and wishing I was back at the café, wishing I hadn't ever stood up or said nothing at all.

I smoked a few cigarettes and watched two old boys shoot eight-ball and listened to them talk about some woman. I don't know who the woman was, but they was both getting with her while her husband was at the mill. They started talking about how she liked it and what she'd do to them and let them do to her.

When I got home, I went in and washed up and then laid down on the bed. After a while, Susan come in and laid down beside me and told me she loved me and I was the only man she had ever loved or ever would. And then W.D. come busting into the room and jumped on top of us, and him and me wrestled and pretended to fight for a minute, and then we all laid back again, W.D. laying in between us.

But then that same evening when we went in for supper I seen this plastic flower laying on the counter—a yellow rose that had the word *Galveston* printed along one of the petals. Susan seen me looking at it, and she said Charlie Ross had left it on the table next to his tip, and so she had brought it on home, but she said she'd have put it in the trash if it hadn't been a flower.

I knew how much she loved flowers, and I said it was all right. I had to admit it was pretty, but at the same time I knew that it was the only plastic flower in the house, since up till now Susan never had cared for them.

I reckon one of the proudest days of my life was when W.D. started the first grade. Susan had spent a lot of time planning out what his school clothes would be, not that it was anything fancy, just regular shirts and pants, but on that first day she dressed him up in his best clothes. He had on a pair of black pants and a white shirt with a stiff collar that bothered the fool out of him and a new pair of black shoes that he said rubbed his heels wrong.

She had gone out and bought him some school things too, like pencils and paper and a notebook. We found out later on that they liked for the little ones to use these special big pencils that their fingers could hold onto better, but we didn't know about that right at first.

Susan did know some things though. She'd talked to other women in the mill village and she'd found out about the teachers and what they was supposed to be like. And she found out about what W.D. would have to eat if he ate what they fed him in the lunchroom there, and she decided she'd let him go on and try it, since he was such a picky eater anyhow. She reckoned he was just as likely to eat what they fed him as anything she'd sent along. Turned out he liked them school meals. Ate things at school he never would have touched at home. Developed a liking for vienna sausages. Started eating rice and meatballs and spaghetti and plain loaf bread with cold butter on it.

But other things about school caused him a problem. At the end of the first week, he come home and went off into the back of the house and started to cry. I wasn't there, but Susan told me about it. Said she went in and asked him what the matter was, but he wouldn't say. He crawled up in her lap and started to suck on his thumb, like he hadn't done in years. She held him and rocked him for a while, and after she could tell he'd settled down some, she asked him again what the matter was. He told her he couldn't read. She told him couldn't nobody read when they started out and that he could do just as good as any of them other children in the first grade. She explained to him how it took a while to learn to read and that you just had to go one letter at a time.

When I come home that day, there was big letters everywhere. Susan had cut great big letters—some of them two feet high—out of paper and cardboard, and she had painted them different colors and stuck them all over things in the house and out in the yard, and she had pasted them on herself and on W.D. too. When I walked in, they was both laughing. W.D. run over and put a big yellow *D* on me, clipped it to my shirt with a clothespin. There was a *T* on the table and a *S* on the stove and a *F* on the floor and so on. They'd had fun cutting out the letters and finding things to put them on, even though the *X* and the *Z* had them pretty much stumped.

After that, W.D. didn't have no trouble at all, and he got to where he really liked going to school. Turned out he was one of the best readers in his grade.

But I keep on going back to that first day, a cool morning for early September in Georgia, maybe because it had come a big rain the night before. There was a little breeze, and the sky was clear blue, and the sun shining. Both me and Susan walked W.D. over to the schoolhouse, which was not in the mill village but on the other side of Jackson Street, the main road that cut through Red Oak. I remember feeling that it had all happened too quick, that it couldn't be time for W.D. to be going off to school, since it seemed like yesterday that Mrs. Gasaway drove us to the hospital in that rainstorm.

W.D. kept running out ahead of us. He'd run a little and then stop and walk for a stretch, like maybe he'd remembered how he had promised to behave. He yelled back at us and told us to come on, but we were moving slow that morning, in no particular hurry to hand our boy over to the county, walking along letting the minutes stretch out and looking around us at where we were at and where we was headed and at our baby boy up ahead of us, who was not a baby no more.

Turned out we got to the school early anyhow, and they hadn't let the children in yet. But the parents could go into the school and speak to the teacher if they wanted to. So we left W.D. out on the playground and went inside and spoke to this Mrs. Buford, who was going to be W.D.'s teacher. There was another child's mother there. Mrs. Buford told us she was looking forward to having Wheelus in her room, which did give us something to say, and we told her we called him W.D., and then she said she would too, and she wrote it down.

We went on back outside because by then it was about time for the bell to ring and for W.D. to be going in. We looked out across the playground till we found W.D. Susan said, "Well I swan. Would you look yonder?"

W.D. was barefooted, his feet and the bottoms of his pants legs covered with red dirt, and his rear end too where he'd sat down. And where he'd got his hands dirty, it looked like he'd rubbed them on his shirt front and left streaks of red dirt across his white shirt and on the thighs of his pants. I pointed out to Susan where his new shoes was laying, along with his notebook spread wide open and facedown next to the shoes, like he'd just slung it there.

W.D. was racing another boy for one of the swings. He got there first and jumped into the swing so it twisted and went sideways and almost went over into the path of another swing going back and forth about as high as a swing can. Susan was about to head down to the swings and snatch him bald-headed when the bell rung, and he run over towards his shoes and his notebook. We walked over there and Susan grabbed him up and popped him hard on his bottom three or four times and asked him didn't he know she'd got him all dressed up in these good clothes so he'd look nice on the first day of school. "And look at you now," she said. When she spanked him, he started to cry a little, but she didn't pay him no mind. She knocked the dirt out of his shoes and put them on him. Then she grabbed him up and took him over to the spigot at the side of the schoolhouse and she wet down a handkerchief and washed him off as good as she could. Washed some of the dirt off his clothes, washed it off his face, got his shirt all tucked in good, got his hair combed. I picked up the notebook and shook the dirt out of it.

By the time she got through fixing up W.D., the last bell had done rung, and so it turned out that he was late for his first school day. We walked him in and took him on down to his room, and Susan apologized to Mrs. Buford, who was already talking to the children, but she just smiled big when she seen W.D., and she said it wasn't no problem at all.

Susan and me, we got to laughing about it even before we'd got out of the schoolyard. I said, "Give him two more minutes, he'd have had that shirt off."

Susan said, "Well it ain't funny," but she was leaning over against me, with both her hands wrapped around the upper part of my arm when she said that, and she couldn't hardly get the words out for laughing.

We went up the little rise that takes a turn just before you go across Jackson Street, and from there we had a good look at the school and the playground down below us. When we got to the top of that rise, we looked back again. Susan pointed out the windows where W.D.'s room was. They had pulled the blinds down and closed them. I remember feeling like we'd done something wrong, leaving him down there, but I only felt it for just a second, since I knew it was the right thing to do, and not only that, it was the law. And even after the way he had showed out and messed up his clothes and been late on his first day, I was still proud of him. I knew he'd do fine.

Next to the schoolhouse there was about a quarter acre of bare dirt where the playground sat, and where minutes before there had been children running wild and climbing all over the slide and the swings and the jungle gym and the seesaw. Now everything sat dead still. Something that looked like a cap laid on the ground beside the swings, which hung down on their chains, not moving. You could see the places under the swings where feet had scooped out the dirt. And the seesaw had one end on the ground and the other one pointing up.

We kept walking, but I looked back one more time at W.D.'s window, and when I did that, right then the sun hit the glass and it flared up and blinded me for a step before I turned away and went on.

15

I'm a plain-looking man, and it's always surprised me that any woman would ever want to have anything to do with me, especially a woman with Susan's looks. What me and Susan had, there wasn't nothing else like it, and I always knew how lucky I was, and I wasn't about to do nothing to mess it up.

At the mill I worked pretty much on my own, fixing looms. Didn't have to talk to a lot of folks. I ain't saying I wouldn't speak to nobody, but I didn't ever go out of my way. In the weave shop, folks mouthed words to one another or made signs with their hands, but I almost never did.

One day this new woman come on as a weaver, and she started looking at me a lot and smiling. I smiled back at her. Then she waved me over, and walking towards her, I thought she must have had a problem with one of her machines, but when I got there I seen it was personal. She just straight out asked me to come over to her place after work. Said she had some beer back there and she'd be happy to share it with me. She had her hand hooked inside my belt when she said this, and she got right in my ear to make herself heard.

I told her thank you, but I couldn't. I said I was a married man and I didn't drink, but I told her I appreciated it. I thought that would have took care of the situation, but she just kept on, like what I said didn't make no difference. She said I didn't look like a man that would let his wife tell him what to do, and besides, she said, she wasn't asking me over for nothing but a cold drink and it didn't have to be a alcoholic drink either. She said she hadn't made no friends yet, and she was just trying to be neighborly. She got up to my ear again. "And I'll make you the best neighbor you *ever* had, sugar."

I went on back to work. Renfroe was across the room and he seen what happened, and he come over there laughing and winking at me, and asking me what I was up to. I had to laugh myself, but I told him I wasn't up to nothing. Said that old girl over there had got some ideas in her head about her and me, but that I didn't know why, and that I didn't want to have nothing to do with her.

There's some men that's got to have them a lot of women, but Susan was always more than enough for me, from the day I met her. There's women that need a lot of men too, and maybe this woman was one of them.

Anyway, I didn't plan on having nothing else to do with her, didn't even plan on talking to her, and for about a week I didn't, till one day she followed me out on my break. She had to have followed me pretty close, since she couldn't have found me if she hadn't. I had me a private spot I'd go to on my break sometimes. It was down in the basement on the other side of the machine shop.

Wasn't nothing there except a little dead-end corner where a few things was stored, but where there was a open spot right at the end. It was cool and quiet, and instead of standing around talking with folks on my break, sometimes I'd come down there. I'd pull me in a crate to sit on, and I'd smoke a cigarette and just sit there, or I might spread a bundle of cloth on the floor and lay down for a few minutes. I got to where I could sleep for ten minutes and wake up right on time.

This particular day I had laid down and fell right to sleep, and she just slipped her body on top of me, real easy-like, and I woke up tasting her mouth, and for about half a thought I believed it was Susan, since lots of nights we'd turn to one another still partways in a dream, and so I reckon I moved towards this woman like I wanted her.

But then I woke up, and I said, "God Almighty, woman," and she started putting her hands all over me, and she put her mouth on mine again. I twisted out from under her and sat up, and I said, "I can't do this. I done told you that."

She leaned over and kissed me real soft, and she said, "But you didn't mean it," and as quick as that, it was like something popped loose inside me, and I kissed her, and she was laying herself back on the cloth and pulling me down when I heard steps, and I let her go and stood up and stepped out past the boxes to see who it was. I seen Foy Pirkle walk by on his way to the machine shop, but I don't believe he ever knew I was there.

I turned around and looked at the woman, and I said, "I got to get back to work," and I went on upstairs, with the taste of her still in my mouth.

I never had nothing else to do with the woman, never touched her again. She tried talking to me, but I wouldn't answer her. I quit going down to the basement on my break.

When I got home that day, I felt like Susan could see it in my face, what had happened, but things went on like always. I felt bad about it, but I figured I'd be a fool to tell her, and then one day I come home and went in the bedroom and I looked up on the chest of drawers and noticed that the yellow rose Susan kept there in a little vase had another plastic flower beside it. This one was a big sunflower, and it had a name printed on it too; it said *Wichita* across the middle of it, in red letters.

16

Sometimes I eat in the dining room when I'm working at the nursing home, and that's one way I've met some of the folks. The first day I ate there, I sat with Jimmy Pooler, who ain't but about forty-five. He's paralyzed. They roll him up to the table and put him sideways to it, so his left arm's right at his plate. He can make little moves with his fingers to let the aide who's feeding him know what he wants a bite of next. There ain't a thing wrong with Jimmy's mind, and the aides, they all like to feed him and so forth because he makes them laugh. It's kind of like a private joke though.

That first day when I sat down there across from him and the aide, she was laughing up a storm right when I walked over. I just smiled at them and asked could I sit there, and Jimmy said, "Hold the phone, Pedro, you got a ticket?"

I sat on down, since I was already halfway in the chair when I asked, and I said, "What's that?"

"You got your ticket?"

"What ticket?" I said, looking over at the aide. She smiled but didn't say nothing.

His eyes went over toward her too, and he said, "What ticket?" He moved his eyes back to me. "Man, don't you know you can't eat without a ticket?"

I knew he was having fun with me, but I didn't know what I ought to do exactly, and I looked over at the aide and I said, "I don't know nothing about no ticket."

She said, "Don't tell *me*."

I looked back at Jimmy and I said, "What kind of ticket?"

He said, "On sale right here. Look in my shirt pocket."

I'd about had enough foolishness, but I went on anyway and stood up and walked around and looked in his shirt pocket, and sure enough, there was some pieces of paper and written on each one of them was *Wolf Ticket*.

I read it out loud, and then Jimmy and the aide—her name was Cecilia—and some folks at the next table all busted out laughing, and I couldn't help but laugh too when I seen how he'd played a trick on me. I knew about folks selling wolf tickets, but I hadn't ever had nobody sell me an actual ticket, and one they'd gone to the trouble of printing up and carrying around.

I took one ticket and I said, "How much?"

"Fifty dollars," Jimmy said.

I held up a nickel and dropped it in his shirt pocket. "Here's my first payment," I said, and that set him off laughing again.

He said, "Sit down, man. Just don't try to steal my girl."

Cecilia slapped him on the back of his hand and said, "Don't you be telling this man I'm your girl. The way you treat me?"

But Jimmy was already moving his finger towards his plate again, and Cecilia cut him a little piece of pork chop. She raised it to his mouth, and he took it in and chewed it for a long time. I went ahead and started eating.

After a few more bites, Jimmy said, "I got to get me a motorcycle." He slanted his eyes over at me. "You know where I can get me one?"

"Well," I said, "there's places."

He slanted his eyes towards Cecilia. "Man said there's places. Hell, I know there's places. I need me a special motorcycle, one you can drive with your eye muscles and your mouth and one finger. I give you my check, you think you can find me one?"

I figured he liked to talk that way and so I just went along with it. "You sure you don't want a airplane? Get you one of them jets?"

"Now you got it," he said. "Eyes go one way, the jet turns. Eyes go another way, it turns again. Puff on a tube, that baby climbs. Suck on it, you go into a dive. Yeah, you got it. Hey, forget that motorcycle. Get me a jet." He winked at Cecilia. She shook her head and raised another bite of pork chop, waiting for him to stop laughing before she put it in his mouth.

To this day, me and Jimmy have never had a serious talk. We always joke and carry on like that's the only way to go.

Pete went out one morning and come home with a story to tell. He'd gone to the service over at the Catholic church, and then he drove on out in the country, like he does sometimes. Said he went around Gratis way and then up past Bold Springs and then got lost and somehow ended up on the south side of Monroe, over by the mill, almost out of gas. He pulled up to a little store with gas pumps outside and put a few dollars worth in the tank and went inside to pay for it. There was a woman in front of him at the counter and it looked like she'd done all her grocery shopping for the week at that little store, since she had bags all over the counter and down at her feet. Pete said he could look at her and tell she was one of them Mexicans that had started to show up in town.

She had a little boy with her, about five years old. He grabbed up one of the bags and started to carry it out. The bag was so tall he couldn't see where he was going, and so he tipped the bag to the side and a can fell out and Pete picked it up and put it back in.

The woman looked at Pete and said, "Thank you," and then looked away real quick. The man at the counter helped her load up the rest of the bags into her arms—there was three big bags— and then he stepped out from behind the counter and opened the door for her and the boy, and they went out.

Pete paid for his gas and bought him a soft drink and stood there and talked to the man at the counter while he drank it. They was both of them shaking their heads about last night's baseball game on the television, where the Braves had lost in the last inning after being up by two runs. The man said he thought the players made way too much money and that was part of the problem—made them lazy, he said, since they was all millionaires. Pete halfway agreed with him, and they kicked it around a little bit, till Pete finished his drink and went out and drove off.

Down the road about a quarter-mile he come up on the woman and the boy. It looked like the bag that the boy was carrying had ripped open and that it had only just happened, since Pete could see a can rolling across the road, and the woman squatting, trying to set down her three bags without spilling them, which she couldn't do, and two of them tipped over.

Pete, he slowed down and pulled his car up alongside of them and said, "Need some help?"

The woman looked up, at the same time picking up boxes and cans real fast and putting them back in the bag, and she shook her head no and kept shaking it and looked out of the corner of her eye at the boy, who started to shake his head too.

Pete pulled the car off onto the shoulder of the road, cut the engine and got out. I can imagine how he might have made the woman and the boy uneasy when they seen him getting out and walking towards them, since Pete's bad back makes him move and turn all stiff-like, makes him look right strange. He walked into the road and picked up a can that had rolled onto the far lane, and then he walked back and held it out to the woman. She took it without looking him in the face and kept on gathering her groceries, which Pete started to do too.

She did look at him then, and it was a sharp look. She had just about got everything picked up, had put the torn bag in the boy's arms and then laid things in his arms one after another, so he cradled them loose, trying to hold them together as best he could with the bag. Then she went over to the other bags and squatted down and tried to get all three of them in her arms and stand up at the same time, and she almost had it, but then one bag slipped out as she raised up. It hit the ground and fell over and spilled some things out, and she went down on one knee.

Pete bent down and held the woman by the elbow while she stood up, and then he picked up what had spilled, put it back in the bag, and then helped her get it positioned between the other two bags she was holding.

"Thank you," she said, "thank you"—Pete figured that was all the English she knew—and then she said something to the boy and they started down the road again.

"I wish you'd let me give you a ride," he said. He was speaking real slow and exact and sort of loud and pointing at the car.

The woman shook her head again, and they took a few steps and just as they got even with the front of the car, the load that the boy was carrying come apart in his arms and went every which way on the roadside. When that happened, the woman slumped sideways over onto the hood of the car and one of her bags fell against the windshield, and as she went to pick it up again, she looked over into the car, and Pete said she seen that statue he keeps on his dashboard—he said he seen her look right at it—and then she said something to herself that he didn't understand, and she started to try to get the bags back into her arms.

But then Pete picked up the bag that had fell over against the windshield, and he went around and opened the trunk and put it in. Then he come back and got the other two bags and after that, him and the boy rounded up what was spilled everywhere and they dumped it loose into the trunk.

The woman just stood watching them, and when they'd put all the groceries in the car, she and the boy got in the back seat and Pete got in the front and they drove off.

Pete said, "Tell me when I need to turn, O.K.?" and he looked back at the woman, and she said, "Yes."

They didn't have far to go—just past the mill, on the east side of it, one street over. When they drove by the mill, the boy leaned out the window and shouted, "Papa," and waved at the brick building, even though there was nobody outside it and all the windows was bricked up.

The woman said, "Rolando," calling the boy down, and he sat back.

"Your husband work there?" Pete asked.

"Yes." The woman answered real quick, sort of took Pete by surprise the way she come back, after her being so closemouthed.

He figured she understood more English than he'd thought, and he wanted to ask her some things, but before he could, she told him to stop there. They'd come down a side street, past a swampy field and a burned-out building, and then up to this big old run-down house with a balcony that wrapped around it but slanted like it was about to fall. It was the only house on the street. Pete said there was music coming out of it so loud that when they got all the groceries from the trunk, and after the woman had thanked him again, she said something else to him but he couldn't hear enough to understand, and before he could ask her what she said, her and the boy had gone on inside.

When Pete told me what happened, I could tell he felt good about being able to help them folks, even though when he told it, like always he had to throw in some complaining—made out like he'd been in a hurry to get back home and they'd slowed him down, and now he was wore out, he said, even though he didn't look it to me.

But that ain't the end of the story. It turned out that Pete run into them again one Sunday morning at the Catholic church service. He seen them sitting off to the side of him—the woman and the little boy and a man and two other children, two girls, both of them older than the boy. He looked over there and the woman looked back at about the same time and they both turned away. But then Pete looked again and he seen the woman whispering to the man, and after she quit whispering, the hard look on the man's face changed and he give a little nod towards Pete, and Pete nodded back.

He had a mind to speak to them when the service was over, but he didn't, since when they turned to go out, they stopped to talk to another family that looked like Mexicans too, and he decided not to break in on them.

The first day they used me as a janitor at the nursing home I went in nearly every room, getting the trash and the dirty bedclothes and so forth.

There's all kinds of folks in there—young and old, crippled and strong, some that remember every day of their life and others that don't know you from one day to the next. Like you got Jimmy Pooler, and you got Mrs. Barton, and you got Horace Thompson and you got Susan, all worlds apart from one another.

Jimmy I done told you about. Mrs. Barton, she's about ninety, and she thinks every man that comes into her room is her daddy. She'll say to me, "Daddy, I'm mad at you," and I'll say, "Why's that, Mrs. Barton?" and she'll say, "You were mean to Janie," which is the baby doll she holds onto twenty-four hours a day. I'll tell her I'm sorry, but it don't matter, because don't nothing much register with her. She calls me daddy every time I go in there, and all she cares about is that doll, that doll and the food they give her, which she can't stand. Most of the times when I go in there, it's to clean up food off the floor where she's dumped it.

Horace Thompson ain't got no reason to be in the nursing home at all except that he's outlived everybody, outlived his wife and their daughter and his brothers and sisters. Never had no grandchildren, and so he's about as alone in the world as you can get, but there ain't a thing wrong with him except that he's broke, and he's so old won't nobody give him a job. I reckon he's close to

Mrs. Barton's age, but he could probably beat a man twenty years younger in a footrace.

And it seems to me his mind must work like a movie camera. The reason I say that is that he can remember things there ain't no reason to remember. He'll tell you things like what color dress the woman was wearing who sold him a tin of shoe polish at a drugstore over in Claxton back in 1937, and he'll remember—I swear he will—how long he used that tin of polish, and then when he run out, where he bought his next one. Little things like that. It's right peculiar is what it is.

And Susan, she's just the opposite, even though she's a good bit younger. She's got that Allheimer disease, or whatever you call it, and her mind is pretty much gone, and she forgets everything. She can be right clear about what she's looking at and what she's thinking of at just that minute, but even then, she's likely to get all caught up in something she can't let go of, and she'll worry it to death. They say sometimes she starts yelling for them to come get somebody out of her room, and it'll turn out to be her, looking in her mirror.

Some folks have visitors and some don't. Mrs. Barton's got pictures of family lined up all across her dresser and on her night table, and there's a stream of folks come in to see her just about every day, and they always come get her and take her to somebody's house on holidays, even though she don't know what's going on.

Jimmy Pooler has this one woman that comes in to see him. He does have a brother too, but I only seen him one time. This woman comes in right often, and she'll sit there with him and put his cigarette in his mouth for him and take it out, and every time she's there he'll make her laugh, get her rocking and doubling over. But I've seen her cry too, and when she gets like that, Jimmy

134

holds his head real still and looks past her like she ain't even there. His face don't look mad or sad or nothing, but just like he's somewhere else.

Susan and Horace Thompson don't ever have the first visitor, but it don't seem to bother her at all. Like I said, she gets her mind all caught up in something and won't let go of it, and usually what it is is that for some reason she thinks that something is going to happen tomorrow, and she's looking forward to it, and she wants to be ready for it. Just what it is, she can't ever say, and exactly how she needs to get ready for it, that ain't real clear either. She's got a few dresses in her closet, and she'll want somebody that's come into her room to take them out and hold them up so she can decide on which one she's going to wear tomorrow, wherever it is she's going. She's had me do that for her every now and then, and she always decides on the same one—always this black dress—but then she don't remember nothing about it the next day or even later on the same day, and she might want to do it all over again.

One day after I started cutting the grass there, Horace Thompson come up to me while I was sitting on the steps out back, taking me a break. I didn't know who he was then, but he just started talking and told me all about the place—the names of all the folks living there, where they come from, what shape they was in, and so on.

And then he got off talking about the past. Like I said, he can almost paint you a picture, since he'll tell everything—what a place looked like and smelled like—and it'll be about as real as what's going on right then.

I been thinking about things a lot lately. By that I mean actual things, like you can see or hold or look at, the way you can't do with an idea, say, or a memory. I been thinking this way mostly because of Pete, since he's a Catholic, and it turns out Catholics are big on actual things. I never knew that, but then I never spent no time with anybody that was a Catholic either. Pete says he ain't a hard-line Catholic himself, but he still is one.

A while back, he got to talking about it. He said he had a uncle that swore he had bought him a piece of the cross they hung Jesus on, the actual cross. I hadn't ever heard of such a thing, and I told Pete I had a hard time believing it could really be a piece of the cross, since wood just don't last that long out in the air, and besides, I said, how would you ever know where it come from? They could have just picked up any old piece of wood and sold it.

Pete allowed he didn't put much stock in that piece of wood neither. But then he went on and talked some about things that did matter to him, like them beads he uses for saying prayers. Talked about what all them beads stand for. And then he got to talking about how different a Catholic church is from a Baptist or a Methodist church. Go in a Baptist church, he said, you might as well be in a courthouse or a schoolroom. No statues, no pictures, no candles that mean anything, no holy water, no confession booth, none of that.

I'd always heard about Catholics going to confession, and so when he mentioned it I asked him what it was, and he told me, and then after that he got off talking about how they took the Lord's Supper.

I broke in and told him how we done it in the churches I'd gone to—how the deacons would pass out them little shot glasses of grape juice to everybody, and then they'd pass around a plate full of pieces of soda cracker, and everybody would take one, and after the preacher said some things, we'd all drink the grape juice and eat the piece of soda cracker.

Pete thought it was real funny, what I told him, but then he turned serious. He said the Lord's Supper wasn't nothing to fool around with. He said Catholics, when they drink the wine—and it's real wine—and when they eat the little wafer thing, they believe it turns into the real blood and the real body of Jesus. I said I didn't see how they could think so. He said they did all right. I asked him did it taste like blood, and he wanted to know what kind of question was that.

So I've been thinking about how it is to be a Catholic, with them beads and medals and such, and about how it is to be a Baptist, where you've just got the Bible and there ain't nothing between you and God, nothing to stop you or help you out either, with no way to know whether you've got right with God except to go to the book and pray and then do it all over again the next time.

Sometimes I do wish I had me something to hold on to, like Pete does, but the things he believes in—his beads and his candles and his wine—they don't mean nothing to me and they never will, even though every now and then, out of nowhere, there it is, and I can taste it on my tongue, and it's blood, and I know whose it is.

17

Uncle Mack said something was going to happen. He come to the house all excited and wouldn't sit down. He'd just left Hodges Store, where him and a group of men had been sitting around listening to Mr. Stillwell go on about what ought to be done to the boys that busted into his house. They never touched his daughter—and Mr. Stillwell was loud on this point, Uncle Mack said—never laid a hand on her, but they could have, and so it looked like some folks thought they did, and that was something she'd have to carry the rest of her life, he said—folks whispering what happened to her. Said no black niggers had a right to be there in Alice's bedroom, and somebody needed to teach them a lesson.

Uncle Mack said the men started to tell stories about what had been done to niggers that violated white women. He was fixing to tell them to us too, but Mama told him we didn't want to hear it and that it was time for him to go, and he did. But first he stood his ground and just stared at her, looked her up and down like he'd forgot she was his dead brother's wife, or like it didn't matter to him no more, if it ever did. All his talk had worked him up into a lather. His spit had got all cheesy in the corners of his mouth, and he'd started to sort of flick out his tongue when he talked, and he'd stop what he was saying and just smile at Mama.

Seeing him look like that at my mama made something rise up in me that I hadn't ever felt before. I knew right then if he laid a hand on her I had it in me to go after him with the butcher knife that was laying on the kitchen table not two steps away from where I was standing. I knew it as sure as I knew anything.

But I didn't have to. He headed for the door, and before he went out, he turned and said, "The Judge has got it in his head it was some niggers from right close by that done it, and he's aiming to find out, and he wants me to help him."

The next morning Isaiah come over to the house and knocked on the back door, and when Mama opened it he asked her was there anything special she needed done that morning. Said him and two of the girls would be out there picking cotton, said the girls and maybe Ezekiel would be helping out most of the day, but that he had some things he had to tend to over in Yellow Shoals, and so if she needed anything special he'd like to go on and do it right then.

Isaiah come to the house every day to ask Mama did she need something. He told me one time Essie Mae told him she didn't want Mama worrying more than she had to, wanted her to know there'd always be somebody coming by to check up on us and see did we need something. Didn't want Mama to have to go asking, day after day.

That day, like most days, Mama told him no but thanked him, and then he made his way across the yard and on out into the field. I got my sack and went on out there with him.

Picking cotton was the only thing I ever seen Isaiah do fast. He'd bend down and start his long arms working, and he wouldn't raise up till he got to the end of the row, and there wasn't no way I could keep up with him. That morning, while we picked, I told him what Uncle Mack had said. We'd done talked about what happened at Mr. Stillwell's house the day after it happened, when everybody first heard about it. Seemed like we'd both heard the same story, and there wasn't much else to say, and we'd just let it go. But when I told him what Uncle Mack had said, there was a part of it he hadn't heard yet—how people had started saying the black boys had took advantage of Alice, and she was probably carrying a baby and so forth.

Isaiah's hands stopped and he raised straight up and said "They saying the boys jump on her?"

"They saying that, but it ain't so." I said. "Alice says it ain't, and Mr. Stillwell too."

He bent over again and went to picking fast. I said Uncle Mack told us Mr. Stillwell was talking about making a example out of the boys when he caught them. I told him Mr. Stillwell thought it was somebody from pretty near by that done it, and that they'd better all be on the lookout because he was going to be coming around and Uncle Mack was coming with him.

Isaiah didn't raise up another time till he got done, and by then he'd gone off and left me anyhow, so I'd have had to shout if I wanted to talk to him. And before the morning was over, I seen him headed down the road toward Yellow Shoals.

That morning, right about when me and Isaiah was talking about Uncle Mack, Uncle Mack showed up over at the Cutts place by himself. He showed up over there drunk and carrying a shotgun. Come up on the porch with that shotgun and held it on Ruth, who was Isaiah's special sister, the slow one. She was by herself at the house, everybody else being out in the field. Uncle Mack pointed the shotgun at her and asked her how many boys there was in the family. She started crying and tried to run in the house, but he grabbed her and made her sit down on the porch, and he asked her again how many brothers she had. She couldn't count them, but she told him their names. There was Isaiah, Ezra, and Ezekiel. Uncle Mack asked her where they was at right then. She said that Isaiah and Ezekiel was working, but that Ezra was way off somewhere hiding out because he'd got hurt bad, and that her mama had told her not to talk about it.

Isaiah had walked into Yellow Shoals to buy something at the feed store, and then he headed back towards home. Just below town, when he come to the Dempsey place, he left the road and started to follow the creek back, like me and him used to do. Old man Dempsey was out on his porch that day, and he seen Isaiah go off through the woods towards the creek.

There wasn't no mystery to why Yellow Shoals had the name it did. Just south of town the creek curved and kicked up a little white water right in the middle of the stream. And in the shallows just below, where the rocks come up out of the water, for some reason they had a bleached-out look, and when the sun hit them just right they had a yellow look to them, almost gold. Along the creek bank next to the rocks there was a sandy clearing, and sometimes folks from the town would come down there to have picnics by the water. There was a trail that cut over to that clearing from the main road, left off right at the Dempsey place.

Some things it's hard to explain. Like one time when I had a dream that lightning struck Mozell Tukes's white milk barn, and then the next day lightning hit right beside it and killed one of his cows. And like the time when I went down to that revival to get healed, what happened to me on the road that cut through Cozy Town. Both times, and others—I know everybody has them; there ain't nothing special about me—I felt like I was part of something that come to visit me from the outside, like I didn't have nothing to do with it.

That's a good Bible word, *visit*. I looked it up one Sunday afternoon when everybody else was out in the yard or in the dayroom spending time with whoever had come to see them, and I was alone in my cell with my Bible and my other book. That same word can mean both the best and the worst things that can happen to you. The Bible talks in a good many places about the Lord visiting to comfort people and make them strong and save them.

But then there's that other kind of visiting, where he's come down to bring revenge and to curse and to destroy, like it says in Exodus: "for I the Lord thy God am a jealous God, visiting the iniquity of the fathers upon the children."

And I *have* felt visited in my time, whether by the Lord or in some other way. I've been caught up and pulled along, and I've come to places I didn't have no idea I was headed for and which I never would have tried to get to on my own.

It was a school day, but I didn't hardly ever go to school no more. That day I went and seen Alice there, it was the first time I had been in a week, and school had only just started, so I'd already missed most of it. And then too, time had come to pick cotton, and even when I could go to school regular, back when my daddy was alive, I'd take off to help out with the picking. And so I wasn't in school that day, but for some reason I'd been thinking about it a lot. The middle of the afternoon, about time for school to be letting out, I got to thinking about the other children walking home, and how I'd be walking home too right then if it wasn't cotton-picking time and if my daddy was still alive. I got to wondering about Alice. I got to thinking about how she used to come past me and wave at me.

And I thought about how good it used to seem sometimes to get away by myself right after school, after I'd been in the middle of folks all day. About how I used to walk a ways down the road and then turn off and follow the creek home. Out at the creek sometimes I'd think about how, while I'd been at that schoolhouse — with the teacher talking and students whispering and paper rattling and doors whining open and shut and footsteps going down the hall—out there at the creek, things had been going on real quiet, without nobody there to see them. How what was so important back at the schoolhouse, it might still be important, but it was as different as night and day from the way it felt being out at the creek, which could seem like the only place in the world.

I set my sack down right there where I was at. There was acres yet to pick, and a lot of daylight left, and the others was still working. I just walked off, like I was plain worthless, which right then maybe I was. But I was hot and my back ached and I couldn't see no end to what I was doing, since I figured I'd be picking cotton or scratching in some other man's dirt for the rest of my life. And over yonder somewhere, girls and boys walked along talking and joking with one another, talking with one another about things that didn't have nothing to do with me, like I wasn't even living.

Everybody has places in their life that they go back to in their mind over and over, and that cotton field is one for me. I know now that the longer you live, the more simple and the more complicated your life gets. I can't explain that, but I know it's true. When you go back to those places, to days you've held onto for so long, they'll be clearer and simpler, like the pure truth. And then too, the older you get and the more you understand, you won't be exactly the same person looking back, and simple things will change and get more complicated.

I see myself out in that field—a boy without shoes, and with a cotton sack at his feet. A skinny boy wearing overalls he's outgrown, so the pants reach halfway up his calves. A boy standing there like a weed, standing up straight under the sun. And when I see myself that way, it's the same boy I've always known, and the boy I partly still am, even this old.

That boy comes back to me, bringing with him the cotton field and his own shadow he can see against the dirt, and the blue sky reaching almost to the road where it cuts through the pines, and I see him set down his cotton sack, and I see him start out for the creek.

18

I've never been big on the sorts of things like you'll see in movies, where there's two people in love and the whole story is how there ain't nobody else in the world for either one of them. I don't think the world works that way, don't think it's even anywhere close. You find somebody to love like Susan and me did each other, you're just plain lucky. The world goes on regardless. It don't plan and it don't care. It don't even notice.

I'd spent time with other women before, and I knew a little bit about them, enough to know how different Susan was. Sometimes a woman will know what's going on when a man won't, and there are women that will use that against a man to get what they want, turn him every which way without him really knowing it. Susan never was that sort.

And there's women too that don't want to be nothing except some man's woman, but Susan couldn't have lived that way. She had her own ideas and her own work, and none of it hinged on me.

I said I didn't believe in those stories like they have in the movies, and I don't, but that's mainly because I don't think the world fixes itself to suit folks. It don't set up a neat little story for you to play out, and if you think it does, you're on the road to some sad times.

On the other hand, it might really be true that I could have traveled all over the place and never found nobody like Susan. And that's pretty much what I've come to believe now, whether it matters or not.

When I'd take my break, sometimes I'd go outside and sit on the loading dock and light up a cigarette and lean back against the bricks, and I could feel Susan there with me. I'd get that good heavy feeling you get in your bones when you been working hard. I'd draw in the smoke and it would ease me down. I'd sit there looking at the rocks and gravel shining out in the street, looking at the clouds go by, and I'd think about Susan.

I didn't like holding things back from her, things that I knew put space between us, and I hadn't ever talked with her about my spells. I'd had them when she was around, but I'd always been able to hide them. I'd feel one coming on and I'd go off into the bathroom or somewhere I could be by myself.

One Sunday night after we'd come back from church—it was the next day after we'd gone up to Atlanta with Renfroe and his family to see the Atlanta Crackers play—we put W.D. to bed and then we sat in the glider out on the front porch and I told her about my spells. How they'd hit me just about any time and there wouldn't be nothing I could do to stop them, how I'd feel sick and weak and about to blow up inside but paralyzed, and I told her how scared I got.

I told her I'd been to the doctors, and about how they'd done all them tests but couldn't find nothing, and that I had pretty much give up on doctors, but how it didn't really matter now, since I hadn't had a spell in a long time. I told her about the time I went down to Mt. Zion and heard Brother Oakley preach and seen him heal some folks and not heal others. I told her about the little deaf boy that didn't get healed and how he stuck out his tongue at me and laughed when I looked back at him. I don't know why I told her about that.

I was fixing to tell her about how sometimes now I'd feel a spell coming over me, and how it would die away, and then before I could tell her about what happened to me that night on the road that cut through Cozy Town, before I could tell her about Yellow Shoals, she said, "Let me tell you something." She put both her hands over on mine, and I quit rocking the glider, so the little squeak it made stopped, and all I could hear was the crickets and the tree frogs out there past the light. "I been waiting a long time for you to talk to me about whatever it is."

It made me want to pull away when she said that, maybe because what I thought was a pure secret wasn't, and I felt kind of foolish, but she held onto me.

"I knew there was something when you went down to Mt. Zion to see that faith healer and then you come home and didn't tell me. Alma's friend Charlene Connor, she was over there that evening, and she seen you, and then Alma mentioned it to me. I figured you had your own reasons for going, and you'd tell me if you needed to."

What hit me right then was that it seemed like Susan knew how you was supposed to love somebody, where maybe I didn't.

I looked at her and nodded my head and felt my throat closing up on me. I looked away and coughed, and when I turned back to Susan, I seen W.D. in her. Usually it's the other way around: you'll see the mama or daddy's face in the child's. But just then I seen W.D.'s pretty little face in Susan's—the same dark eyes looking at me the way his did sometimes, like I couldn't do nothing wrong, which was a foolish way to feel, and Susan sure knew better than that. But there it was in her eyes.

Somebody in Bull Watson's house turned off a light, and then another one. I watched the smoke from my cigarette drift up and disappear. I noticed how clear the stars were that evening, just like they'd been the night before, when we was coming back from that ball game in Atlanta. I asked Susan did she remember how, right after we met, we used to sit out and look at the stars and she'd ask all them big questions.

"I still feel like it sometimes," she said, "but I guess I just keep it to myself."

I put out my cigarette and lit up another one. I pushed off with one foot, and we moved back and forth a little in the glider, and I started telling her about what happened one afternoon when I was fourteen years old and I was out in the field picking cotton, and I just quit, put down my sack and went off walking toward the creek.

I told her how I could have done something, could have said something, but I didn't. I stayed hid off in the trees, and then I crawled on my belly up to where I could see what was going on. I seen Mr. Stillwell, and Uncle Mack, and the sheriff, and a man everybody called Goat, and two other men I'd seen before but didn't know the names of. Isaiah was down in the sand on one knee, and there was blood running from out of his left ear. He wobbled when he tried to stand up, but then he did, stood up and tried to walk off, and I heard Mr. Stillwell say, "Just hold it right there." But Isaiah took another step, and Mr. Stillwell swung his rifle butt and caught Isaiah smack in the mouth and he went down and stayed down.

Then Mr. Stillwell went over to his truck and got a long whip out of it and started to hit Isaiah with it. He tried to crawl out of the way, and they let him. Isaiah twisted and rolled on the sand, and the sand stuck to the blood running out of his ear and from his mouth and nose, and coming through his shirt. He reached the creek and rolled over into it, and when he done that, the men drug him out, laughing and whooping. It's hard to remember now just what they said because they was all yelling and laughing at the same time, but I remember clear as day that one voice because I knew it so well and because it sounded something like my daddy's. Only I never heard come into my daddy's voice what I heard in that other one—a kind of high, mean giggle. It was Uncle Mack I heard cussing and giggling, and I seen him squirming around like he was about to wet his pants.

"Where you think you going, nigger?" he said, and he had Isaiah around the leg, and he drug him out of the creek, and he hit him in the stomach with his rifle butt once they had him up on the sand good. "Why don't you answer me? Boy, didn't your folks teach you no better?" he said, and he kicked Isaiah in between his legs, and then Mr. Stillwell waved the others off and started in on him again with the whip.

The sheriff stayed off to one side, standing by the truck, with his arms folded, and he never said nothing the whole time, just stood there and sort of frowned.

Just the sound of that whip could make you jump, and every time it hit Isaiah, the men yelled, and the whip whistled when it cut through the air coming down. That's a sound I used to hear in my sleep—that whip whistling and popping and the shouts and

Uncle Mack giggling and then what come out of Isaiah's throat, which wasn't nothing for a long time. And then he started to let out his breath hard when they hit him, and then he started to moan, and then that broke down into a cry, and inside that cry when he could get it out he started to say, "Please, sir" and that's all he ever said the whole time, just "Please, sir."

Mr. Stillwell swung the whip hard, and then he dropped it and whirled around, holding his shoulder. "God Almighty damn," he said, and he went over beside the sheriff and bent over, holding onto his arm, and then when he raised up again he looked even madder than before.

When he dropped the whip, the other men jumped to get it, and Goat come up with it, and he went to whipping Isaiah like a crazy man, swung so wild he missed him twice and hit the sand, but he caught Isaiah good four or five times.

Mr. Stillwell said, "Y'all strip him down buck naked."

Isaiah's clothes was soaked with blood and all cut up by the whip, at least the shirt was. The whip hadn't cut through his overalls, but you could tell how he was bleeding under them from the way they stuck to his body.

When I dreamed about it later on, this was where I'd start to feel like I was having a spell in my sleep, when they started to take Isaiah's clothes off. I can't hardly talk about it, even now; them taking off all his clothes and leaving him out there naked on the sand was worse to me than anything, even beating him half to death like they'd already done. There's Isaiah laying out there like that, helpless to do anything about it, unless somebody was to help him, and there wasn't nobody around to help him.

Isaiah curled up sideways and put his hands down between his legs.

149

Mr. Stillwell said, "Y'all get hold of him. Get his arms and legs and stretch them out," and they grabbed him and pulled his arms and legs apart, and Mr. Stillwell come over there, still holding his arm, and grabbed a rifle laying on the sand, and he swung it like he was chopping wood. Held the rifle halfway down the barrel and brought the butt up over his shoulder and swung it down hard four times, hitting Isaiah between the legs, until his privates looked like a mess of red persimmons you'd smushed under your foot.

Isaiah went to howling then, and I want to say he screamed like a animal, but the truth is, it wasn't like no animal I ever heard.

Mr. Stillwell turned around and walked off toward the truck, and he said, "Somebody shut that nigger up," and Uncle Mack went over to Isaiah and swung his shotgun hard against the back of his head, and Isaiah stopped screaming and laid there still. You might have thought he was dead, except for the way he breathed hard and every now and then sort of trembled and twitched and his legs kicked out.

The men walked over to the truck and had them a smoke. From where I laid, I couldn't make out what they said, but I could hear them talking low—Uncle Mack talking, and Mr. Stillwell shaking his head from side to side. I laid my head down on the pine needles and closed my eyes, and I could still hear them. I laid there, and then the strangest thing happened to me. My heart was beating so hard in my ears, it seemed like the men should have been able to hear it, and I'd never been so mad in my life— though mainly I was scared, scared till I felt sick, like my whole body was sick. And then I fell asleep. How that could be, I don't know. Scared to death and I fell asleep. I woke up when I heard somebody say, "Whoa there."

I raised my head and I seen Isaiah crawling towards the creek and the men coming after him. I seen Isaiah crawling on his knees and his elbows. Blood was dripping out from under him, and it made a trail in the sand. The men just walked over there casual. They knew he wasn't going nowhere. Goat put his foot up against Isaiah's ribs and pushed him over. Didn't kick him but just pushed, and right then you could see how weak Isaiah was, since he fell over sideways.

It took him a while, but he got back up on his elbows and knees and crawled on towards the creek, and they let him go. He reached the creek and got all the way in the water, right where there was a deep spot in the shoals, and it looked like it sort of woke him up, and his arms started to flapping like he was trying to swim, and that drew some laughs from the men.

"Lord have mercy," Mr. Stillwell said, laughing and shaking his head. "Now I've seen it all."

Uncle Mack had hold of Isaiah's ankle, and he laughed that high giggle, and he said, "He's a swimmer, ain't he? Watch him go."

Isaiah's arms slapped hard against the water right after Uncle Mack said that, and the men thought it was real funny, and I reckon that got Uncle Mack fired up, and he started talking to Isaiah, got right over at his ear, and he kept on looking back up at the men.

"Boy, you better swim if you can, because we ain't through with you yet."

Isaiah just held still in the water. Then he laid his left side over on a rock, and Uncle Mack come down on his right side.

"And we ain't through with the rest of your folks neither," Uncle Mack said. "And we might even let you watch it. I'm gonna get me a piece of that little one, the one that ain't right in the head, the one I seen over there this morning. Get me some of that little heifer and see how she likes it. And she'll like it all right. Never seen a nigger girl that didn't. After I get it in her, won't be long before she'll be twitching and moaning and talking that monkey talk and telling me to come on, and she'll be . . ."

Isaiah grabbed Uncle Mack by the back of the neck and now Uncle Mack's head was in the water. Isaiah braced against the rock on his left side and pushed Uncle Mack down under with his right arm, and Uncle Mack's legs kicked out from behind him and his arms went splashing around him, and then the men fell on Isaiah like a pack of dogs, but Isaiah had his big hand locked onto Uncle Mack, and the same right arm that had put down the Big House and everybody else in the county, that same right arm held Uncle Mack under the water.

When the men come at Isaiah, they all sort of fell on top of him and pushed him down under but pushed Uncle Mack down under too, and when they come up, Isaiah still had hold of him and still had his head under water, but Uncle Mack had gone limp. They tried to roll Isaiah over on his back, but he had hold of the rock and I reckon he had some kind of foothold on the bottom, and they couldn't move him.

Then I seen Goat step back and raise his shotgun and shoot Isaiah in the middle of his forehead, and a piece of his head flew off and landed right in front of me and some of the blood got slung up on me, and I couldn't help what happened then. I let a sound come out of my throat and I rolled away and raised up a little and looked back to where the creek had gone red and to where Isaiah laid with half his head shot off and Uncle Mack sat up choking and coughing and Goat still held the shotgun trained on Isaiah like he was fixing to shoot him again. The sheriff had turned around and headed for the truck, and the other men moved off onto the sand.

But Mr. Stillwell didn't move. He stood out in the water with his arms at his side and he sort of slumped over, and he looked straight at where I was laying. It seemed like a long time that he didn't move, just stared. He bit his lips and frowned. I could see Isaiah's blood flowing around Mr. Stillwell's britches legs. Then he turned and yelled at the men, "Y'all come on back here and get this boy," and I was about to break and run when I seen him reach down and grab hold of Isaiah's leg and start to drag him towards the sand.

The men come and got the body, and what I heard later was that a black man found it just this side of Ricksville, about a half mile down a logging road, and the story that went around was that the sheriff thought another black man had killed him over a woman, but they never did arrest nobody.

Wasn't nothing ever the same after that. I had laid there and watched it happen and never moved, never said a word. And whenever I thought about telling somebody, I remembered the sheriff, who'd seen it all and turned his back. I couldn't see how nothing but more trouble would come from me telling some-body—and that's the truth—but the main truth is that I was too scared to open my mouth.

And just about every night that piece of skull would come whirling at me in a dream.

That's when the spells started. The first week or so, it felt like I was caught up in one long spell, even though I was still walk-ing around, still had my legs under me. It was like I was walking around dead and ashamed and scared to die.

I watched Otis and Essie Mae bury Isaiah, and I never opened my mouth. They knew what had gone on anyhow. They didn't need no white boy who just happened to have seen it with his own eyes to come along and tell them who exactly it was that killed their boy. That's what I told myself over and over.

I seen how Otis looked at me when I come over there after Isaiah got killed. His face was sad and hard anyway — it had always been like that — but after they killed Isaiah, his face, at least when he turned it to me, it was sad and hard and I don't know any other way to put it than to say it was ready. Like he was ready to fight mostly, but sometimes I reckon he was ready to cry. And he never said much to me anyway, but afterwards he didn't hardly speak.

James Tukes started coming around their house a lot, and if he seen me there or seen me coming up, he'd cuss me like always, and Essie Mae would tell him to hold his peace, but Otis never said nothing.

They did keep helping us out with the farm, which was mostly Essie Mae's doing. Sent Ezekiel and the girls around, but not as much as before. I never did see Ezra again.

Mama seen I was sick to death, but she didn't know half the reasons, and she couldn't do nothing for me. She knew Isaiah and me was close, and she thought I was grieving over him, but she didn't know what all else had got tied into it.

After all these years, I told Susan, it had come to seem to me like Essie Mae must have had some feeling that I was carrying around more inside me than I let on. She must have seen something. Her own children had lost their brother, and she could see how it weighed them down, how it would start them crying at night sometimes, so she'd get up and go over to them and whisper to them and cradle their heads and just hold them a while before

154

she went on back to bed and did her own crying. She seen her own children and how they suffered, and when she looked at me she must have seen that it wasn't so much grieving as something else. Isaiah was my friend, but he wasn't my brother, and whatever I felt for him, it wasn't like Ezekiel felt, or Martha, not even close. So I think Essie Mae could see there was something else going on with me—that I was hurting in a different and strange way—and she tried to help me out, even in her own awful pain, something I didn't appreciate for a long, long time.

One day when I come over there she sat me down and told me how there'd always been a kind of special feeling between Isaiah and his sister Ruth. Essie Mae said she'd been watching me when I'd be around Ruth and she said every now and then Ruth sort of looked at me like she used to do Isaiah. Said she seen how every now and then I'd make Ruth smile, like Isaiah used to. She asked me would I spend some more time with Ruth when I could, because she thought Ruth would like that and Isaiah would have liked it.

Ruth was ten years old, but she couldn't read or write yet, even though she'd been to school some. One of the things I tried to do was teach her, but I couldn't make it happen. It was like her mind had stopped at about a four-year-old's, and she couldn't ever get past it. So when I spent time with her, we'd play little games, get us some rags and sticks and make us some little people, have them talk to one another and fight and chase one another. We'd play in the dirt, making mud pies and so forth. And we'd play chase and we'd climb trees.

Essie Mae must have known something, because when I was playing with Ruth, it was almost like nothing had ever happened, like I had gone back in time. And I reckon in a way I had, since I was playing children's games again. It helped me out so much that when I'd start to have a spell, sometimes I could think about Ruth's face or try to hear the way she laughed and it would bring me out of it. It didn't happen a lot, but sometimes.

The glider had a squeak to it, a little cricket sound when it went back and forth, and I'd been pushing off with my foot the whole time I'd been telling the story, and now Susan put her hand on my knee and held it still and the sound stopped, and she cried so hard it took me by surprise. I don't know what I expected, but I didn't think it would tear her up like that.

19

I reckon Pete ain't seen either one of his children now for about two and a half years. They got their own families and jobs, and times are pretty hard for them. The daughter, she'll write him a letter or a postcard once a month or so, and they'll both of them call him every now and then, but not regular. The only regular thing about it is the time of day they call, if they do. They'll both of them call him right after suppertime, and before nine o'clock. Never known either one to phone earlier or later, except on Christmas once.

So from about seven to nine o'clock I can see Pete get different. He likes to go for his drive late in the day, but he won't ever be out of the house from seven to nine. And he gets real quiet, and this is while one of the news shows is still on, when he wants to be talking back to the television. Sometimes I catch him looking at the phone, and if it rings, he won't let it ring twice.

Every so often, he'll call them too, but it ain't the same. After they've called him and he hangs up, he'll act like he's just had him two cups of strong coffee—talking and arguing with the television or with me—but if he's the one that called them, after he hangs up, he ain't so lively.

And some nights, when nine o'clock has come and gone he'll get to looking older than he is, like some of the folks I've seen at the nursing home that don't have no hope left. One night he got to looking that way, and we'd sat together not saying nothing for a good while when he up and told me maybe I was lucky not to have ever had no children. I just let him talk.

He said some folks you choose to love and some you don't. He'd chose to love his wife, he said, and he'd loved her true—and after he'd been with her a long time, it was too deep to ever let go—but he said he hadn't decided to love his children. Didn't have no choice about it.

He said it's strange how you start to look at things different when you got children, said this to me real serious, like he was explaining something to me that I didn't know nothing about. He said as long as you only got to worry about yourself and maybe somebody else that's grown and can take care of themselves anyhow, the world looks one way. But let a baby come, and things start to look different. You start to think about the years ahead, when maybe you never did before.

He said that having a child would even make you look back at things in a different way. You can't ever see your mama and daddy the same, he said, once you've got somebody of your own to take care of. You start to realize what they went through, and what all they wanted for you, and maybe why they done some things you always thought was wrong. He said he didn't think he'd ever really seen his own daddy for the man he was till his own baby was born.

I didn't say nothing. After a while Pete got tired, I reckon, and he went on to bed, and I did too. But I laid there a long time and couldn't sleep. I got up and went out on the porch and sat there.

The family across the street was wide awake too. They had all the lights on and the windows open, and I could hear the television and them yelling over it. I heard a girl's voice scream at somebody, "I wish you were dead." And then I heard a man's voice, "*I'll teach you,*" and then the sound of scuffling, and a scraping, like furniture being moved, and then I couldn't stay out there no longer. I went back in the house and closed the door to my room, and I couldn't hear them from there, but by then it didn't matter.

20

That last summer there was a revival at our church, and they brought in this evangelist from over around Savannah somewhere, and all he wanted to preach on was race mixing and how the Bible said real clear it was wrong. He pulled out the old story of Noah and Ham and how God made the children of Ham the servants of everybody else for the rest of time.

The story wasn't nothing new to me. I'd heard lots of folks tell it, including my daddy, explaining why there was a line between black and white you couldn't cross, but I always thought it was a mighty peculiar story. Noah goes and gets drunk and passes out, and then his son Ham wanders in and sees him laying there without no clothes, and that's the reason he's supposed to have been cursed, him and all his children and grandchildren and so on, forever.

I just never could imagine God being that touchy. And I had decided that a lot of them old verses—mostly the ones back near the beginning of the Bible—they didn't need to be paid too much attention to. Like where it says you ain't supposed to eat catfish, that kind of thing.

It seemed to me the separation between black folks and white folks was just something natural, and I believe my daddy felt that way too, mostly. He'd tell the Bible version, but then he'd follow it up by pointing out how animals keep to their own kind—how you don't see sparrows and bluejays setting up house.

Like I said before, Otis Cutts was my daddy's best friend, but you didn't see the two of them sitting down at the table together, or going to the same church, or sending their children to the same school. It wasn't natural, Daddy said. Said folks like Otis understood that too. There was a line.

When that evangelist come to Red Oak, we only went to hear him the first night of the revival, even though it lasted all week and there was children from the church going all over, doing what they called pew-packing—trying to round up folks to sit in their pew. If they filled it up, they won a prize.

Walking home that first night, I told Susan I wasn't going back. "I can't put up with that foolishness" is what I told her, and we just walked on and never did talk about what I meant.

It wasn't all the talk about Ham and race mixing that I couldn't stand—I had my own ideas about that—but the way the evangelist acted. I believed that folks get the call; that they don't just up and decide they want to be a preacher and then go to it. And it seemed to me that evangelist liked being up on the stage too much, and that he didn't have no business preaching.

It was almost like he was up there making fun of preachers too, the way he dressed and carried on, wearing that white suit with a red necktie and a big red handkerchief sticking out of his pocket, and he even had him a bright red Bible. He combed his hair up high, swirled it around, and it shined and it never moved.

It's true that he was one of the best singers I ever heard, to this day. Could have sung on the television. And he made folks laugh, with the different voices he did, and he made them cry, and he cried too.

It was kind of fun to watch him, but it got old quick. And then when he cried I could tell he'd just worked up the tears, like they do in the movies. I could tell it easy. And I thought to myself there's too many real tears being cried for somebody to be going around pretending. And that, on top of him being somewhere between a clown and a stage act and a preacher—the preacher being the least part of it—that got off with me. I told myself before he was half done preaching that I wouldn't be coming back.

Susan seen how disgusted I was when we was walking home, but I never did explain it to her, except for saying that one thing, and so she might have thought I was thinking about one kind of foolishness when I was really thinking about another one.

21

It was Thursday evening of the same week, right about sundown. W.D. was out playing in the yard, and Susan had come back to the house after working in the flower garden. I'd been asleep and was in the kitchen fixing us a bite to eat.

Susan went in the bathroom and stayed in there so long I almost knocked on the door. It was dark when she come out. I'd already called W.D. in, but he'd begged me to let him keep on playing with his toy cars in the driveway till suppertime. The driveway was lit up by the porch light, and I said all right, but told him it wouldn't be long before we'd be calling him in.

When Susan come out, she sat at the kitchen table and watched me do the litle bit of cooking I was doing. I was fixing us a breakfast for supper, something I done pretty regular. I'd scrambled up some eggs with cheese, and I'd fried some ham and made us some redeye gravy to pour over the grits and to sop up with the biscuits.

Susan sat at the table and looked down at her hands, frowning.

I said, "I was beginning to think I was going to have to come see about you."

She give me a weak smile and said, "I'm just moving slow." She took a deep breath and let it out. "I hadn't been feeling too good."

For the first few days after I told her about my spells and about Isaiah, Susan had treated me real gentle. She brought me things, like she might just show up with a glass of lemonade and give it to me. She made me a cake. She'd want to sit beside me and hold my hand. But then she'd changed, got quiet and stopped paying me all that attention, which was fine, since I felt all right and I didn't need her to be doing them things.

Everything was ready to eat now, and I turned off the stove and started to put the food on the table. I said, "I been noticing that. You reckon it's something you ought to go to the doctor about?"

She shook her head. "Where is W.D.?"

"I told him he could stay out a little bit longer. He's in the driveway."

I started to walk out to get him, but she said, "Why don't you wait a minute?"

I could hear the train coming out of that curve off 129. You could always hear it when it had left the mill spur and picked up speed good. First it made a booming sound on the tracks and then as it come toward the crossing you'd hear the whistle. Sometimes you could hear the cars rattle.

"Is there something else the matter?" I asked her.

She stood up and went over to the sink and bent down and washed her face, and then she raised up and turned and leaned with her back against the sink. She was facing my way but looking at the floor. She stayed that way a little bit before she said anything.

"I told you a long time ago how my Aunt Lenora raised me to hold back. A woman's got to keep a good part of herself a secret from anybody else, she used to say, and especially from any man."

I could hear W.D. making a loud engine noise and then making the sound of squealing tires out in the driveway.

"Well, now that you told me the things you did," she said, "maybe there's something *I* need to tell *you*."

I looked at her, and her eyes was so serious and sad in a way that I hadn't ever seen before, and then I knew the day I'd been expecting had come—that this was the day she was going to tell me about Charlie Ross and what she'd gone and done with him.

But I'd thought about it a lot—prayed about it too—and I'd made up my mind, and as far as I was concerned—this is what I told myself, you understand—if she could look me in the eye and swear that whatever happened was all in the past, then we'd just try to let it go. I'd thought a lot too about what almost happened between me and that woman down at the mill, and how it would

162

have gone on and really happened if Foy Pirkle hadn't walked past just when he did. I hadn't ever told Susan about it, and I wasn't going to, but I hadn't ever forgot it either, and so if she had something like that to tell me, I wasn't going to go wild over it. At least that's what I told myself.

The train was rattling off into the dark somewhere past the highway now, and I'd heard the last of it go.

I said, "Is it about Charlie Ross?"

She looked at me and shook her head and her eyes never changed. "No, it ain't Charlie Ross."

She turned back and tightened both knobs on the sink, even though the faucet wasn't dripping, and then she walked over and sat down at the table.

"It ain't Charlie Ross. I'm sorry you even have to ask me that. He did give me a little attention, and maybe I shouldn't have let it go on, but there hadn't ever been anybody but you."

She was telling me the truth. I could hear it in her voice, and I could see it in her eyes.

"No," she said, "it ain't that," and she took a deep breath and let it out. She said, "I hadn't told you the whole truth about some things, and I never did think I would, but now I feel like I want to."

I used to wonder how it could be that one second I'd be a free man, with Susan beside me and W.D. on my lap, and then in another I'd be awake on my back and looking up through the dirty light coming through my cell window.

She said, "You've got to understand that I never knew my mama or my daddy either one. I was raised by my Aunt Lenora and she was the only real folks I ever had. I've seen pictures of my mama and my daddy. My daddy was white."

The Bible says we shall all be changed, in the twinkling of an eye.

"And in the pictures, my mama don't look colored at all, but she was. Her mama and daddy was both supposed to have been real light-skinned, and they say her mama's hair was just like mine."

I used to stand at the razor wire and smell the honeysuckle on the breeze, and all of a sudden I'd feel my legs and arms go heavy and my chest sink in, like all the air was getting sucked out of me.

Susan's mouth kept moving, but I couldn't hear her for looking at her—at her skin and her lips and her hair. Her skin was the same color as mine, the same color. I looked at the little dark hairs on her arms, the brown mole on her neck—just a dot you could barely feel. I looked at her lips, those lips that could always bring me towards her with a move so small nobody else would see it—a little pout or a kiss. And her hair, the hair that made me look again the first time I seen her—hair like black silk, hair I buried my face in every night.

Lord, I looked at her, and there she was, there she was, but she was gone. And in her place there was this idea. And the idea took over, and I felt it come up from deep down, like something swirled up from the bottom of a creek—something rotting and stinking and forgotten down there torn loose by the current so it bobbed up through the surface of bright water; something that wore the pretty leaves already floating up there on its half-eaten skullhead now like new dead skin pasted against it—and I didn't have to think no more, and the idea spoke up and I said, "You just gonna sit there and just like that you gonna tell me I married a nigger?"

I reached down and swept the plates off the table, and they hit the wall, and gravy and eggs splattered everywhere.

164

I heard W.D. say, "Mama?" and Susan was looking at me like I was a man come back from the dead, and she started to stand up and go out to W.D., but I pushed her back down in the chair.

"All these years . . ." My voice come up out of my stomach like vomit. "All these years, and the worst of it—goddamn you to hell, goddamn you—you done made my boy a nigger too, put your own nigger blood in his veins and made him a nigger too. *My* boy, *my* boy."

I heard this shaky voice come through the screen door. "Daddy? Y'all don't. Mama?"

I picked up a chair and slung it against the wall, and there was nothing left to do then but hit her—which I'd never done a single time before in the whole time we'd been together, but I was about to. And I raised my hand and then I heard it through the screen door—the howling on the asphalt and then a little thud, real soft—and Susan and me was out the door and running towards the street, and Mrs. Gasaway, the same woman who drove us to the hospital when W.D. was born, she was getting out of her car.

W.D. was laying off on the shoulder of the street, with his feet on the pavement and his head on the dirt, facedown. When we turned him over, blood run out of his mouth and his nose, and his lips and eyes had puffed up, his lips all blue behind the blood. He was limp as a dishrag.

I picked him up and carried him into the house. When I lifted him, his head twisted sideways in the crook of my arm and when it done that, blood run out of his mouth, and Susan caught his head and held it, but it looked then like his mouth had a little puddle of blood in it.

I laid him down on the sofa. Susan washed some of the blood off his face and tried to clean it out of his mouth and nose, but as soon as she done that, more blood took its place.

Everybody was in the house by then—Renfroe and Alma and Bull Watson and Mrs. Gasaway, everybody shouting and crying, asking was he breathing, said we had to get him breathing. I heard Bull shout, "Breathe, boy."

I heard Mrs. Gasaway's voice choking. "The Lord is my shepherd. I shall not want . . ."

Susan kept on making a sound down in her throat, over and over, like she was about to say *no* but she couldn't get it out, and the sound was coming fast, with every breath she took.

I pushed on W.D.'s chest, and blood spurted up and spread out on his shirt, and it was dark blood now, and a blue knot had swole up on his forehead, and his skin had lost all its natural color. But he was breathing. I put my ear down to his nose and mouth and heard air going in and out, fast and ragged, stopping and starting. "He's breathing," I said, and I kept on saying it.

Then the ambulance was there. They laid W.D. on a stretcher and carried him out, Susan right beside them. Her and Alma both climbed in the back with W.D., and I heard her shout at the driver to go on.

Renfroe yelled at me to get in his car, and I did, and he took off for the hospital. Neither one of us said a thing the whole way. When we got there, we went in the emergency room and seen Alma sitting there by herself, crying. Renfroe went over and sat next to her. I asked her where Susan went, and she pointed at two doors. I started through them but met a nurse who pushed me back and told me I'd have to wait outside. I said, "It's my son," but she told me I'd have to wait there and that she'd let me know how

166

he was. Said it wouldn't do him no good for me to be in there with him, and that I'd just get in the doctor's way.

"Is he dead?" I asked her. "Just tell me, is he dead?"

"No sir, he's not dead," she said. "I know that for a fact." She said his heart was beating when they brought him in, and they'd started to work on him right away, and so he had a good chance.

The nurse had her hand on my back and she was pushing me over towards a chair, and I sat down in it.

Right in front of me there was a picture on the wall. It was a picture of a house and yard. There was a oak tree in the yard, with a swing hanging down from one of the limbs, and whoever painted the picture had put a woman in the swing, and they'd painted a few wildflowers growing up from the ditch right next to the mailbox. Little white flowers.

I kept on looking at it for a long time—how long, I don't know—and then I felt a hand on my shoulder. I looked up and it was Renfroe. His mouth was in a tight line, and he shook his head side to side real quick and squeezed my shoulder, and then he turned and walked off. "I'll be out here," he said, and he went on outside.

Alma was gone too and there wasn't nobody in the room now but me. I looked at the doors they wouldn't let me through before, and I got up and went on through them, running and pushing open doors and yelling for Susan.

Two men come out into the hall, and one of them said, "Wait a minute now, hold on there, buddy, hold on now," and they started towards me, but I run down the hall, calling out Susan's name, and when I turned the corner I seen her down at the far end of the hall, sitting in a chair, bent over, with her face in her hands.

I run towards her, yelling her name, but she didn't move, didn't look up or act like she even heard me, and right when I got to her a door opened and they rolled out a stretcher with a body on it that was covered up, but I could see a shoe sticking out, and I pulled the sheet down and there he was, with a hole cut in his throat and his hands folded together across his chest. I leaned over and touched his face and pulled his head up and cradled it in my left hand, and with my right hand I opened his eyes. They looked glassy and set, like the eyes of a possum run over and laying out in the road.

I laid his head down and I turned towards Susan, and her eyes had the same look, staring straight at the wall in front of her.

One of the men reached down and pulled the sheet up over W.D.'s face, and they started down the hall, rolling the stretcher. Susan turned her head and watched them go, and when they had gone around the corner, she turned to me. "Ain't he pretty?" she said, and her eyes still had that look, and she asked me again, "Ain't he the prettiest thing?"

I stood there and looked at her, and I seen that she wanted me to answer her, and I said, "Lord yes."

And it was like my voice shook her loose and she seen who she was talking to.

"I don't have nothing to say to you but this. I intend to bury him by myself. I don't want you there. You understand me? My boy's dead, and I'll bury him, and then if you ever see me again, it'll be a miracle."

It's crazy, but right then I felt the urge to argue with her about what she'd said—not about me, but about W.D., her calling him dead, saying he was dead.

"But one more thing," she said, "and you need to know it. It ain't all your fault. I'm the one that was the fool. I'm the one that killed my baby, telling you what I did."

She stood up and started past me. I stepped sideways to block her, and what come out of my mouth was "I swear to God, Susan," and I don't even know what I was fixing to say, but when she heard my voice she stopped dead-still and waited till I stepped out of her way, and then she walked off and was gone.

Late that night, when I come home and walked into the yard, that was when it hit me. I heard real voices in the air, and I could feel them in my ear—W.D. making his engine sounds over where his toy cars still laid in the driveway; a low moan coming through the screen door, like there was somebody sick inside. And dust rose up from the dirt driveway and swirled around like it knew what it was doing, and when I took hold of the door, it flinched and pulled back, and the floorboards groaned under my feet.

I struck a match and held it to the curtains in W.D.'s room, and then I lit the bedspread in our room, and I went out on the back porch and got a can of kerosene and walked through the house, slinging it around, and I poured it all over myself, and then I laid down on the sofa, put my head where it was still wet with W.D.'s blood. I put my mouth where it was soaked through, and I sucked it out of the cushion, closed my eyes and sucked my boy's blood out of the sofa cushion, as hard as I could.

And all of a sudden Bull and Renfroe was on top of me, and they pulled me out the door and dragged me down the steps, beating at my pants, which had caught fire, and they slung me into a puddle in the ditch and left me there, and when I looked up I seen that the fire had spread over to the next house, where a new family had just moved in. The houses in the mill village was real close together, and the wind had picked up, and everything was real dry, and the fire spread and it burned that house clean to the ground too.

The woman that lived there with her husband and two children—I hadn't got to know none of them yet—she was burned bad when her nightgown caught fire. She had such bad burns all over her face that later on she got to where she never would go out of the house. When I was at Milledgeville, somebody sent me a letter telling me she'd shot herself in the head.

When they thought everything was over, something exploded out of nowhere—nobody ever said what it was, not to me—and it blinded one of the firemen.

I sat in the ditch and watched it all. There was a crowd out on the street looking at the fire, and later on I heard that people said I'd been sitting there in the ditch laughing, but I don't remember that, and I don't believe it.

22

Out of a six-year, two-month sentence to the state prison at Milledgeville, I served it all—August 1954 to October 1960.

I looked up *hell*, and I seen where in Luke, Jesus told the story of a man named Lazarus, who was a beggar that had gone to heaven, and how there was a rich man who died and went to hell, and how he looked up and seen Lazarus up in heaven with Abraham and he cried out for Abraham to send Lazarus down so he could just dip his finger in water and cool the rich man's tongue. But Abraham said no. Besides, he said, heaven and hell was too far apart, and you couldn't go from one place to the other.

So then the rich man asked him to send Lazarus down to his brothers on earth, who was still alive, to let them know the truth and so they wouldn't end up in hell too. The rich man said he knew they'd listen to a dead man come back to tell them something. But Abraham said he wouldn't do that either.

23

I took a sash off somebody's bathrobe at the state hospital, and I hung myself in a closet, but I didn't die. I don't remember the end of it, only that I didn't die.

After that, they started watching me, and it was harder. I got a piece of glass and cut myself deep on the side of my neck and into my wrists, but it didn't work. So then they tied me down, and all I could do was to beat my head against things. I knew if I hit my nosebone just right, it would go back up into my brain and kill me. I tried to break my neck one time. It might sound funny now, but it wasn't then. I run across the dayroom fast as I could—the big room out where everybody sat around, one that was long enough so I could pick up speed—and I bent my head down and just before I hit the wall I crooked it over as far as I could. I figured it would snap my backbone at the back of my neck, like it would have if I'd fell out of a window and landed with my neck bent like that. But it didn't even knock me out. I run across the room and slammed into the wall, and I heard somebody yell, "Touchdown," and then a few people laughing.

They started giving me them medicines and shocks a whole lot and keeping me tied up, but there's only so much you can do. If a person wants to die, they'll keep on trying to find a way to do it. I started hiding anything I could get my hands on, just anything, and not because I knew what I was going to do with it, but because maybe I could figure something out. I made a split in the side of my mattress, and I put things in there. If they let me out for a walk in the yard, while nobody was looking I'd get me a rock or pick up whatever else I might find on the ground, like a penny or a bobby pin. Or I might just reach down and get me a handful of grass or dirt and carry that back in.

One time I found a long piece of tape, and that give me the idea for how to do it. I figured I'd take whatever I had in my mattress — and some of the stuffing would be good for it too — and I'd roll it up and tape it all up tight into a wad and wet it down good so I could mash it all together and then late one night after everybody was asleep and I was locked in by myself and the attendant was way down the hall somewhere, sitting with his feet up and listening to the radio, I'd stick that wad down my windpipe. I'd get it just the right size so I could wedge it back there and then suck back real hard and it would have bobby pins and straight pins all bent up inside it, and I wouldn't be able to get it out even if I wanted to.

I got it all fixed up, and it was about the size of a pecan, and I went ahead with it — breathed the wad back into my windpipe and almost choked to death, but then I woke up not dead again. After that I just sort of give up on dying for the time being. It would come sooner or later, I decided, and I figured maybe the deal was that I didn't deserve to die yet; maybe I was supposed to keep on living so I could think about everything some more and it could eat me away from the inside out. It ain't exactly true that I quit trying though. I did take a bottle of pills I got my hands on one time, after they had put me over in the prison. It was a full bottle with a long name on it that I can't remember now and didn't know what it meant then, but a doctor had ordered it for somebody and so I figured it might be strong enough to do the job.

And then, after a while, after I had kept on long enough trying to do away with myself, I got to dwelling on my mama. It was the strangest thing. Mama had been dead nearly twenty years by then. She'd caught pneumonia one winter and was gone in a week. I was sixteen years old, and I put her in the dirt beside Daddy.

I got to seeing my mama's face. It would just come to me, like out of the air, and then it would go away. I figured it happened because of the way I'd beat my head on things, and it may have. But I could see her real clear for a while there, and something about seeing her face made me quit trying to kill myself. It wasn't like Mama was talking to me or anything, but she was just there. I only seen her for a little while like that, and her face never did come back. In fact sometimes now, unless I see her in a picture, I can't even call up exactly how she looked.

Later on, when I'd be following one word through the Bible, because it had caught my eye for some reason, there'd be lots of times I'd end up paying attention to something else I come across instead. Like I was looking up the word *mill*, which ain't in the Bible but twice, and I come across this verse in Exodus where it says God was going to kill all the firstborn of the Egyptians, from the Pharaoh on his throne, it says, even to "the firstborn of the maidservant that is behind the mill; and all the firstborn of beasts."

Now this is a famous Bible story, and I already knew it, but it never quite hit me what a strange thing it was. I know they put a whole lot of stock back then in the child that was the first boy child born into the family, and that it had to do with the customs they had and all that sort of thing, but two parts of it struck me as odd. One is that God killed "all the firstborn of Egypt," it says, "both man and beast." Later on, the verses mention the cattle, how God killed off the firstborn of the cattle, but it says it right there, earlier, "all the firstborn, . . . both man and beast," and so if you take the Bible word for word, like some folks do, you've got to think that when the Lord passed over the places that didn't have blood smeared on the sides of a door to protect them, the firstborn of every living thing was killed—the firstborn of dogs and rats and wild hogs, all of them.

And then too, the part about killing the firstborn of common folks, like that woman at the mill—and later on, like it says, the prisoner in the dungeon—folks that didn't have no say-so at all in what the Pharaoh was doing, their children was killed too.

I looked up the word *mercy*, and it took me a few days to get to all the times it was in there, and what stayed with me was how in the Old Testament it has God saying he "will show mercy on whom I will show mercy," and how those same words come back again later on, where Paul is talking to some folks and calling up that same verse. And after he does, Paul says, well, maybe you've got a question about what it means, and then he says, more or less, but if you do, let me ask you this: who do you think you are to be talking back to God?

24

Thirty-five years is almost half my life, but it don't seem that long. It's thirty-five years since I walked out of that prison gate and went on down the road, and there was nobody to care, one way or the other.

There's a few things I learned from being locked up, and this is one of them, but one I only learned when I got out: you ain't free just because they let you go. And there ain't much of a story to tell about what happened after they turned me loose. I didn't move around a lot, only when the job run out, and I had to go somewhere else.

I've had lots of jobs but never went back to a cotton mill, even though I did try it when I come to Monroe. I worked at whatever I could find, and one job was pretty much the same as another one, just like in prison. I've mostly had jobs other folks wouldn't take, like picking peaches and pecans and cleaning bathrooms and kitchens, scrubbing out toilet bowls and working over grease traps.

Before they hired me, somebody would always get around to asking me some questions, and I never did hold back. I told them where I'd been, and it cost me some jobs, but I didn't see no reason to lie.

One time I had a job sweeping out the parking lot behind a grocery store. I hadn't had the job but two days when the place burned down, and they thought I done it, and they locked me up, trying to prove it. This happened down around Fort Valley, and they put me in the county jail there, a ratty, stinking hole—toilets all busted, water smelly and brown, so many folks pushed into a cell you didn't hardly have a place to stretch out good. They kept me there a week and then turned me loose but told me to move on, which I did.

And all this time I've been pretty much by myself, even though I haven't always had to be. When I was living down near Valdosta, I met a woman by the name of Betty Ransom. She was a cook in the same restaurant where I washed dishes, and she was a lively sort, always making other folks laugh. She was about my age, which was around fifty-two then, and she'd kept her figure and her looks. She'd been divorced twice, and she had three grown children who had moved away, so she was by herself.

Betty took a liking to me and asked me to come eat supper out at her trailer, and I went a few times. I could have stayed there with her, could have spent the night if I'd wanted to. After we'd eat, we'd sit on the sofa, and after a while she'd slide over close to me and lay her head on my chest. She kissed me once or twice, I remember, but when she seen I didn't kiss her back, she just re-laxed and laid against me, and we spent some comfortable time that way.

Betty and me never talked about it, why I never spent the night there. We talked about folks at work, and we watched tele-vision some, and then I'd go home. We never got into personal things.

But I thought about it a good bit when I was by myself. I was still a man, still had feelings like a man gets, and Betty was a good-looking woman. It wasn't her, it was me.

It's true that it don't matter how much you love somebody: you either die or you go on without them. But when another woman brought her lips to mine, when I tasted her sweet breath, Susan would come back to me, and then I didn't want to be where I was, but only wanted to be by myself, to let the memories go away and stop hurting me.

Betty was my friend, and that was all right with both of us. Pretty soon I left that job and went over to Cordele, and I worked unloading trucks for this place where they sewed blue jeans, and after that I spent some time in Fitzgerald, doing yard work, and then I moved to Tifton, where I lived for a good many years.

One more thing you learn about when you're locked up is time, and how time is always two things at once. You've got your calen-dar and clock time—and that's always what it is—and then you've got what's inside of you, and that's different.

By the calendar, it was always a long time ago that Susan and W.D. was with me, but by what I had inside me, sometimes it seemed like yesterday.

25

Nearly every time I go in her room, she'll be sitting up in her chair—not a wheelchair, but this easy chair next to her bed—and she'll wave me over and start saying she don't know how she's ever going to get everything ready for tomorrow. I've seen her do that to other folks too—everybody that comes in—but don't everybody pay attention to her like I do. They just walk on by, or they'll tell her it's all right and not to worry, and then they'll go on about their business, which is what I have to do too, sooner or later. But I always stop and sit down and talk to her for however long I can.

One of the things she always wants to know is what the weather is supposed to be like tomorrow. When I first started talking to her and she asked me that, I'd take a guess, but I noticed she kept on being worried about the weather, and so now I try to have me a newspaper with me every morning when I'm working there. What I'll do is I'll take it with me into her room, and when she asks me about the weather for tomorrow, I'll show her what it says there in the paper.

And it don't matter whether it says it's going to rain or whether the sun's going to shine, it makes her happy right then, when she's got some idea about what's coming, good or bad. Her face just lit up the first time I showed her a weather report in the paper. The way she looked at me, the way her eyes changed right then, it tore me up. Her mind is so far gone she can't string one thing together with the next, and so she stares and worries, and then just by accident I was able to find something to make her smile, make her happy for just a minute, and the first time I seen that, it made me feel like crying.

I've tried reading some of the rest of the paper to her too, but she don't want to hear it. Never did tell me directly to stop, but when I tried it the first time, while I was in the middle of a sentence, she said, "There's too much noise in here," and so I shut the door, but then she said it again, and so I quit. I tried it one more time, but she put her hands over her ears, and so now I just show her the weather report for the next day. What I'll do is I'll take the paper in and read the report to her, and then I'll cut out that little weather section and leave it with her. She likes to hold onto it and look at it.

Jimmy Pooler, he's started to tease me about spending so much time with her. He'll yell over at Horace Thompson; he'll say something like "Hey, Horace. Ellis bring you something every day?"

Horace Thompson will play along. "Not me."

"Between you and me," Jimmy will say, talking loud across the dayroom, "I believe he's got him a sweetheart. What you think?"

Horace Thompson usually lets it go, and then Jimmy will say something like "How about it, Ellis? You got a thing for Miss Pruitt?" and he'll laugh like he's going to fall out of his chair.

But Jimmy don't mean nothing by it. It's just his way. Me and him go back and forth all the time anyhow, and he loves to get a rise out of me, and sometimes I'll let him think he's got next to me, even when he hadn't. He picks at me about Miss Pruitt, and I tell him he don't know what he's talking about—don't even

have the first clue—and when I answer him back, that cracks
him up.

The truth ain't as simple as it might seem. And if I was to try to
tell it all, how could I ever find the words to do right by it?

I only wanted to see her again, you understand—just to look at
her, that was all. I wasn't going to bother her. All those years since I
got out of prison I'd lived one day to the next, one job to the next—
and what it was didn't much matter—always knowing she was
gone for good, always being sure that if she had ever wanted to
see me again, she'd have let me know, but knowing she never
would.

I had me a job sweeping up at a truck stop down in Tifton when
I got the letter from the government. At first I couldn't make a bit
of sense out of it, but then I seen what happened. I read the letter
over and over, and then I called the phone number at the top of it.
It was a government office that had to do with getting payments
through Medicaid. Turned out they wanted to know how much
money I made, since my wife was on the Medicaid and they said
you can't be on it unless you don't have no money, and since she
was my wife they had to find out where I was living and to look at
the money I made too.

I told the woman on the phone that I didn't have no wife, but
she said I did, told me where she was, and said it looked like my
wife had lied on the form she filled out a good while back, because when they looked up her Social Security number it showed
a different name from the one she was using, and it showed me as
her husband, even though she'd put down that she hadn't ever
been married.

179

I told them what they needed to know, and then I packed up and caught a bus that morning, found me a room, and for a long time, day after day, walked past the place where she lived. I'd stop for a while and look at it, but I never went in. I only wanted to see her. Not talk to her, not even let her know I was there. I just wanted to look at her.

Then I noticed the grass needed cutting at the place, and I took a chance and asked them about it, and they let me do it, but I worked with my hat pulled down low, so she wouldn't recognize me if she seen me. I respected the fact that she hadn't ever, during all those years, made a single move to see me or talk to me. All I wanted was one good look at her.

But it didn't happen. And then one day I was sitting on the steps out back, resting after I'd cut the grass, and this old man come out and started talking to me, and we talked for a long time, and I didn't even have to ask him no questions. He told me all about the place—the names of the people living there, where they come from, what shape they was in, everything. And this old man, he said she didn't really know nothing about what was going on, said she had that Allheimer disease and was getting worse and didn't nobody ever come see her, and as far as he knew she didn't have nobody.

Pruitt was her maiden name, her daddy's and her Aunt Lenora's name, and it looks like she went back to it when W.D. was killed, only I reckon she never did get her a lawyer and do what it took to end the marriage. That don't mean nothing though. It ended, and it's over.

I call her Miss Pruitt. Never Susan, not one time.

But I couldn't bring myself to walk down the hall and go in her room and look at her. I was partly scared that even as sick as she was she'd recognize me and it would hurt her. And something else told me it was just plain wrong too, whether she knew me or not. I had this feeling that it was almost like digging up a grave—not something that worries the dead person in the least, but still a terrible thing to do.

And then when they made me a part-time janitor I had to go in all the rooms, but even then, right at first I'd duck in with my head down and my hat on and I'd grab the trash can and get out of there without even looking up. All I'd wanted was a look at her, one look, and now I couldn't take it.

Then one evening I was sitting around with Pete, and he was waiting for a phone call, but it never did come. He usually just kept on watching television, but this time he turned the set off. He asked me if I minded. I said I didn't. We sat there a long time, not saying a thing, and then I just started telling him, and I told him everything—about W.D. and Susan and Isaiah, and me being in prison, and about where Susan was now and what I was doing in Monroe, and about how I couldn't bring myself to look at her. I told it all, things I'd never said out loud, and it felt strange, but I couldn't keep it in.

After I was done, he started telling his own story, like he hadn't even heard mine. He started to talk about his wife and how much he missed her. Said he never knew how quick the world could change until she had her heart attack. It happened one day while he was at work, and they called him on the phone and told him she was dead, just like that. Nothing for him to say or do. He said he told them, "I'll be right there," and then when he hung up the phone, he thought how foolish that was, since his wife was dead now and he didn't have no reason to hurry.

He said for a long time he never did dream about her, but then he started to. He'd see her sitting there beside him with nothing special happening, and he'd believe she was alive. She wouldn't ever talk though, and sometimes in the dream he'd speak to her but she wouldn't ever answer back.

He'd get this crazy feeling when he woke up, like he could go back in the dream and get her, like the world he'd just been dreaming about was as real as this one, and he could be with her again if he could only get back to it. He said sometimes the feeling would stay with him the whole morning, but that while it was there, and then right after it went away, it made him real sad, like he ought to be able to reach out and get it, but he couldn't, and it was his own fault that he couldn't. That got next to him, and he started to drink a lot of wine at night, so he wouldn't remember his dreams. But when he did that, he felt bad too, in a different sort of way.

Then one night she talked to him. Called him by his secret name, the one they only used between them—Pete didn't tell me what it was—and she told him he'd hurt her feelings, told him he didn't ever look at her pictures no more, and she pulled one out of her pocketbook, and she asked him why he didn't ever look at that one. But it was a picture of somebody else that she showed him, and it didn't bear the least resemblance to her. She asked him again why he didn't ever look at it, and he told her because he hadn't ever seen it before, and right then she pulled the picture away and looked at it hard and then started to laugh and said he was right, it wasn't her, said she didn't have the first idea who it was. She laughed till she cried, right there in the dream, and Pete laughed that way too.

He said when he woke up the next morning he felt like he used to when he was a boy after he'd been to church and he'd feel clean and good inside. He'd walk out of the church and just look at things—the way a tree flashed in the wind, or how a cat followed him with its eyes—and it would come over him that the world was a mystery and it would always be that way, and he wouldn't ever know but a little part of it, not ever in his life.

Pete said the dream changed him. And maybe it was something that just come to him for no reason, he said, out of nowhere, or maybe it was grace. And then he went on and told me that maybe the Lord had give me a gift too by letting me know where Susan was. He said, "Maybe it's a kind of grace, Ellis. You never know." And when he said that, I didn't want to talk to him no more, and I didn't, not that night. Here he'd told me a story that come straight out of his gut—I could see that—and then he'd gone and tacked God onto the end of it, and that part of what he said sounded as fake and as made-up to me as just about every sermon I've heard in my entire life.

The next evening he asked me did I go in and see her that day, and I told him no, and he said I was the most hardheaded man he'd ever run into. "And here's the worst part," he said, "you're so damned proud of it."

"I never should've told you," I said, and I left the house and walked off down the road, not even knowing where I was headed, kept walking and ended up over at the cotton mill.

I stood there looking at the mill and listening to it hum. Every now and then, when a door opened, I'd hear a sharp whirring sound I recognized as spinning frames. I watched steam coming through a vent and rising through a yellow light high up on the wall. I seen folks sitting outside on their break, smoking and talking, and I walked around and went in through the back gate where it was chained loose enough for me to get through, and I walked over to the building and laid my forehead against it and put the palms of my hands flat on the wall and felt the warm bricks and how the mill trembled and shook, and I stayed standing like that for a long time. I felt tired down to the marrow of my bones, and after a while I didn't know whether it was me trembling or the mill wall I was spread out against, like I was either trying to hold it up or push it down.

I walked back home a different way. About two blocks over from the mill, I turned down a street I hadn't ever been on before. On one side of the street there was a swampy field, and on the other side a burned-out building with a fence around it. I seen busted glass everywhere, shining under the full moon. Just past the burnt building, there was a stretch of pines, and then I come up on this house, the only house on the street, a two-story frame house that must have been somebody's fine home once. It had a long porch and a balcony upstairs that wrapped around to the side of the house but that slanted down now, like it was about to fall. The front door and all the windows stood wide open, not a light on anywhere, and I could hear the music blaring. I'd heard it even before I turned onto the street, and it got louder and louder till I could feel it on my skin when I was right in front of the house. Mostly horns and drums, played with a fast beat. And then a voice started up, singing in some foreign language. The music was turned up so loud it seemed like the voice was right in my ear. The singer was at the edge of crying, but he didn't cry. He sung ragged and smooth at the same time, and his voice rose and fell with the horns and the drums.

I walked on, and even when I couldn't hear the music no more, it kept going on in my head, and even though I couldn't say the words, it felt like I almost knew what the man was singing about. I knew how he felt.

I didn't even know I was going to do it, but the next day I went in her room and stood there looking straight at her, and she looked back at me with them dead eyes and asked me to see was there a black dress in the closet, and I got it out for her, and she said she believed she'd wear it tomorrow.

26

It was about twelve years ago when I went back to Yellow Shoals and found out it wasn't there. Ricksville had spread out and swallowed it up, so you couldn't even tell there was a separate town called Yellow Shoals.

I got lost driving around, since they had messed up the roads, tore up the main highway, and run a stretch of the interstate across what used to be Mr. Stillwell's land. His big house ain't even there no more, and as best as I can figure, what sits there now is one of them roadside tourist shops where they sell peanuts and honey and corncob pipes and pieces of cotton they've sealed up in plastic bags, and where they've got signs with little easy words misspelled on purpose.

It's hard to tell, but it looks like where the truck stop sits is where our house used to be. The roads are turned around, the land's graded, the trees cut down, and there just ain't no way to tell. Everything's fenced off too, and so you can't just go out walking anywhere you want to.

But I didn't come back to just look around. I come back to see could I find the Cutts family, so I could talk to them and see what happened to them, but I don't know what I was thinking. Wasn't no Cutts in the telephone book.

And what was I going to say? Was I going to waltz back in after almost fifty years and act like I had a story to tell that could make some kind of difference? I don't know. Maybe I was. Maybe it would have made a difference. But I couldn't find nobody. If I'd found Ezra or Martha or even Ruth, then maybe I would have gone on with it and told it to the new sheriff or the police or somebody, but without them, it didn't make no sense.

I was fourteen when I seen them kill Isaiah, and sixty-two when I went back to Yellow Shoals, and it was gone, along with everybody and everything I knew about the place. The church and graveyard where Mama and Daddy was buried—Missionary Baptist—they wasn't even there no more. Instead, there was a car wash that had gone out of business. Couldn't nobody tell me where they moved all the graves to. I reckon I could have found out, could have gone to the courthouse in Ricksville and asked somebody, but I didn't have the heart for it.

I did drive on into the middle of Ricksville though, and I stopped at this place and got me something to eat, sat there by myself in a booth and drunk coffee for a long time and looked at the faces of the folks that come in and out, like I could recognize somebody, but I never did, and after a while I got to feeling like a fool.

But I sat there some more, and I got to thinking about Otis and Essie Mae, and how they went on with their lives after Isaiah was killed. I thought about how I was only a boy when it happened, and how I didn't have the first idea, not really, of the heartache they had to be going through; and how back then I thought I did though, since I'd lost my daddy, and since Isaiah was my good friend.

What I know now is that unless you've lost a son or a daughter of your own, you can't know what it's like, can't even begin to know it.

It hit me while I was sitting there in that booth that what I felt when W.D. died was what they felt when Isaiah died. A simple enough thing to understand, I reckon, but it had never come to me that way before—it just never had—and when the young black

186

woman come over to the table to refill my coffee cup, she must have seen my face, even though I had turned away toward the window, and she filled my cup and then she patted my shoulder when she left me and went on back behind the counter.

I did find the creek though, since there was a bridge where the interstate went over it. I parked my car on the shoulder and climbed down the bank and followed the creek, and all of a sudden, before I had gone a hundred yards, I knew exactly where I was, and I kept walking, and then there I was, at the shoals that the sun used to turn gold when I was a boy; at the bend in the creek where the water took Isaiah's blood away with it. The same stretch of sand was still there, where they beat Isaiah half to death, and out in the current, the same rock he was braced against when a shotgun took the top of his head off, and up the bank was the spot where I laid and watched it all. I went up there and stood, and I looked down at the creek, and I seen how the big rock kicked up a little white water at its left edge, like it always had; how the water churned and made the same old shape over and over; how fifty years hadn't made no difference at all. And I stood there a good while, waiting for the rocks to turn gold.

27

My daddy used to say you can't love a thing, only a person. He didn't want me to say I loved Mama's chocolate pie, but only that I liked it. Didn't want me to say I loved how the honeysuckle smelled or that I'd love to be able to just lay in bed in the morning and not have to go out into the fields. He didn't believe you could love the land or money or the country, or even things like the truth.

"There's things you like and want, things you admire and feel real close to and faithful to, and such as that" he said, "but you don't love them. You love your mama."

I did love my mama, and I loved him, and I loved Susan and W.D., and there was a time when I would have said I loved Isaiah, but I can't say it now.

All my life I've pretty much used the word the way he said to, but now I wonder.

What if the past is gone and the future cut down to a few hours? So a woman's love for her own child is lost in her confused brain, but it's still there, moving inside her somehow and looking for some way to be what it was? What if you see something in her eyes, just a flash that comes and goes away? And what if you see it when it don't make no sense? Like when she sees the color blue on the weather map in the newspaper, or when she gets a drink of cold water, but not when a picture of her child is held up to her— some old photograph pulled out of a wallet, a picture with one end cropped off, one figure cut out, so that what she's looking at is a woman and a little boy.

Maybe that boy has gone into the color blue now. Maybe he's gone into that cold water.

I do what I can, and it's nothing.

I clean up what she's spilled or knocked over. I carry out her dirty bedclothes. I bring her a piece of that bittersweet chocolate she don't even know she's partial to till it's in her mouth. I take the black dress out of the closet and show it to her. Last week when it stormed and the rain was beating at the windows and it scared her, I closed the door partway and sat beside her and held her hand till I heard somebody coming in.

I bring her flowers off the roadside and out of the woods, and can't either one of us say what they are now, except pretty.

But I know this and I hold it in my heart like the last and maybe the only true promise of my life: if the day ever comes when she looks at me like she's woke up, even if it's just for a second, and she knows who I am, and she calls my name and I hear in how she says it that she don't want me there—on that day I'll go home and pack my things. On that day I'll know what it is that I've been given to do.

28

Last night Pete and me drove down to the Dairy Queen in his old Chevy. It was about ten o'clock and the ball game on TV was already over, and he wanted to get him a milkshake, and so I went along with him and got me one too. The whole way there and back he talked about the ball game, played it all over again, right up to the last out, just like I hadn't sat there with him and watched it.

While we drove home, I noticed how clear the stars were and I started thinking back to that summer when everybody in the mill was talking about the Atlanta Crackers, who was at the top of the league and looked like they'd win it that year.

I wasn't really a baseball fan. Didn't have nothing against it; I just didn't bother with it. But after folks talked the way they was doing down at the mill—and Renfroe would go on and on about some of the players, who he knew all about: batting averages, hits, home runs, and such—I started to read some of the sports page myself when I bought the Atlanta paper. I got to where I recognized some of the names he talked about in the box scores, and I seen what they was all excited about.

So one day Renfroe got this idea. We'd send off and get us good tickets, and then we'd pack up Susan and Alma and Jerry and W.D. and we'd drive up to Atlanta in his car and go to the Ponce de Leon Ball Park and see us a Crackers game. Only problem was that the mill run six days a week, and that meant we'd have to go up on a Sunday, and didn't neither one of us want to do that. But then Renfroe remembered there was a Saturday coming up about three weeks off when they'd told us we wasn't going to work because they had to shut the whole mill for some kind of inventory. We'd got mad about it when they told us, since it meant we'd lose pay.

He sent off and got the tickets and we was all set. W.D. and Jerry got all excited and started to play ball in the yard more than they usually did. They mostly liked to play cowboys and Indians and to run imaginary races with their toy cars. They was both seven years old then, and they didn't catch or hit too good yet, but they had a lot of fun throwing and chasing. And Susan and Alma was excited too. They'd got the trip planned so we'd leave real early, way before we needed to, so we'd get up there in time for us to go by the Rich's store for them to do some shopping. And that's the way it turned out too. The game didn't start till two o'clock, but we was on Highway 129 not long after the sun come up, and then we was stuck in that store for close to three hours, waiting on them women to come on. At one point, W.D. just laid down flat on the floor face down and spread his arms out, and I remember wishing I could do the same thing, because that's exactly how I felt. I was used to working two shifts, sixteen hours of hard labor, but this shopping and waiting liked to wore me slap out.

But finally we got to the ballpark. Renfroe had got us good seats on the third-base line, about twelve rows up, so we looked right down on the Crackers' dugout. The place was almost full. There was two levels of seats that wrapped around behind home plate, and then there was bleachers that stretched out down both foul lines. Off in right field there was one section reserved for the blacks, and it was full too. Home-run distance wasn't too far in right, but you had to hit it over three levels of signboard. It was farther to the fence in left, and I remember there was this big magnolia tree, must have been about five hundred feet from home plate, out in straight center.

I liked just looking at the field, how level and clean it was, the greenest grass I believe I'd ever seen; the way they'd marked everything off so straight with chalk—the foul lines, the batter's box, and the coaches' boxes. The players threw baseballs every bit as white as the chalk.

I'd been to some ball games before, but never in Atlanta, and I'd never seen nothing like this. I could tell just from watching them warming up, throwing back and forth, that we was going to see some real baseball. I hadn't ever seen nobody throw so hard or heard a glove pop like that.

I looked around and I seen Renfroe sitting there like somebody had put a spell on him. I seen W.D. and Jerry concentrating hard on their Cracker Jacks and Co-Colas, and Susan and Alma sitting there talking to each other the same way they would have done on the front porch at home, paying no mind to the players warming up.

We hadn't got there in time to see the teams take batting practice, and that was one of the things Renfroe had planned on, and it kind of got off with him that the shopping run long and we missed it. So we didn't get to see any hitting till the game started, but when we did, it got everybody's attention, women and children too. You hear the bat crack like that, you can't help but look. The way they could hit it, and the way the ball rose and curved, it was hard to believe.

The Crackers was playing Birmingham, and it was a good game, real close right to the last inning, the score going back and forth. When it was tied up in the seventh inning, we bought us one more round of hot dogs and Co-Colas, and I remember sitting back in my seat and looking around me at where I was at and feeling like I was a king. And then in the ninth inning the Crackers' main home-run hitter, a player named Montag, he hit a ball so hard and so far over the signboards out there in right field it seemed like it never would come down. I never seen nothing like it, before or since. It won the game. Folks went wild. W.D. thought it was funny the way I shouted, and I put him up on my shoulders.

There was a train trestle that sat up over the right field signboards, and a freight car sitting up there on the trestle the whole time the game was going on. It had its door swung wide open and I seen a man sitting in the doorway. I noticed him early in the game, and I seen how when something happened, he'd jump up and shout and wave his arms. I started looking out there to see what he would do, even though there wasn't nothing real unusual about him being there. He'd just got my attention. I kept on looking back at him, and then I happened to look up there right before Montag hit that home run, and I noticed the man was gone, and that struck me as curious—why somebody would leave then, when everything wasn't over yet. I looked up there and all I seen was this dark square in the side of the boxcar where he'd been sitting.

After the game we got caught up in the traffic, and it took us forever to get out of there. When we hit one stretch, a few miles out, the road followed a ridge and turned us traveling east for a ways, and you could look to the side and see the city down below us.

Everybody was tired and real quiet. Me and Susan sat in the back seat, and W.D. stretched out on top of us, with his head in Susan's lap. We hit the dark stretches of 129 and started making good time. Every now and then we'd pass a store all lit up or a house with a bright yard light, and the light flashed across us and I could see W.D.'s face. He was dead to the world. After a while I seen Susan was asleep too. It was a hot night, and we had all the windows rolled down, and about a hour down the road we hit a stretch where it had rained, and there was a thin mist on the highway, and you could hear the tires crackling on the pavement and making a whispery sound. The rain had turned the air sweet, and it smelled like some kind of wild tea, made out of weeds and dirt and cut with the smell of hot asphalt cooled off. And you could smell the wildflowers, and you could tell it when we passed a cornfield, the way the air got sharp; you could smell the cow manure and the cotton poison. And a tin roof would flare up in the headlights and disappear; the lights would flash off broken glass by the road and catch the windowpanes of houses in the curves. We got behind a old truck for a while that had a chain hanging down, so it scraped the road and kicked up sparks.

Susan had shifted over and laid her head on my shoulder, and I could tell she was awake now by her breathing. I put my arm around her, and I could smell her hair. Jerry was laid over against Alma in the front seat and Renfroe was up there in charge, and there wasn't nothing for me to do but sit back.

I looked at the sparks that old truck kicked up, and I noticed how, just past them, over the dark ridge of pine trees, you could see the stars—the truck sparks flickering up and dying before you could blink your eyes, and the stars out there so old you couldn't even think about them, not really, but you could see them both at the same time—the sparks coming off the road and dying out, and the stars that could last forever—and there I was, rolling out through the countryside, breathing air made sweet by the rain, with Susan's head on my shoulder, and with W.D. laid across us, gone off in his dreams—whatever they might have been.

And I felt like I could wake up any time and all of it be *my* dream, but I was wide awake, and I was holding on to the ones I loved, and we were going home.

Rembrant
Dunlop
City Lips
Crest